I FELT A FUNERAL, IN MY BRAIN

I FELT A FUNERAL, IN MY BRAIN

WILL WALTON

PUSH

Library of C on Data
availa
ISBN 9
10 9 2
Printe
First
Book d

For Tyler

CONTENTS

"Have you the little chest—to put the alive—in?"

Emily Dickinson

START

I turned in the response when it was due, on the last day of school. It was just an "effort" thing, you know. It could be whatever. Five extra-credit points on the final, as long as you turned it in. *Respond to one work of literature we studied over the course of this year.* Nothing serious, or it wasn't meant to be. But I kept thinking about Vardaman and that one-sentence chapter from *As I Lay Dying*—"My mother is fish"—and I couldn't stop myself—I tried very hard. I worked on it all night.

When the final was over, we were all just sitting at our desks. Ms. Poss walked to the front of the room.

I figure we'll start here:

Ms. Poss: "Class, I am in *love* with this response here, listen. One of you has penned a <u>poem</u> inspired by *As I Lay Dying*. It's called 'I'll Never Eat Fish-Eggs and Why,' and I bet y'all will pick up on the reference to Vardaman's famous chapter—shh, class!—the one with the famous 'My mother is a fish' sentence—quiet now!—I'll read it to y'all."

Ms. Poss (*clearing her throat*): " 'I am vegetarian. I make no exceptions for fish-eggs, no— / though fish-eggs, some argue, is, was, were, depends / are you be, will you be, have you been / eating them? If so, will soon— / Once hardly, if ever, was truly a fish.

" 'My mother is a fish, or so she / drinks, I mean / "thinks." / We aquarium on weekends together, and she believes / they are our ancestors / Pink, bright

2

blue, and yellow slippers— / "We were bright-colored like that too once," she says.' "

Someone fake snoring.

"Stop that now! Have some respect! 'My mother is a vegetarian. / My grandpa is a fisherman. / So that is complicated. / At family dinners, our plated ancestors / my mother and I both, staring down at ours. / And my grandpa's longtime girlfriend is there / like a grandmother / insists / "Eat! *Eat!*" / My mother says we were bright-colored like that too, once.' "

With Ms. Poss reading it aloud, the whole thing felt much longer than I thought it would feel.

I mean, I had spent the whole night working on the poem. But on the page, once I printed it, it had turned out to be so short-looking—disappointing really— all that work and so much feeling, for it to turn out to be so small.

But then, when Ms. Poss was reading it out loud, it had felt like it might never end. It was the worst of both worlds really. I felt flattered that she liked it, or at least that it stood out amid the other responses. But some people were laughing, so I also felt embarrassed about that. They didn't know it was me, but I was sitting right there.

And then Luca, who was looking right over at me, like he'd known all along—maybe he had.

If you knew me at all, you might know it was me. But Luca was the only one who really knew me.

"I can't believe you had the balls to write about her drinking like, I mean, what if Ms. Poss had decided to, like—" Luca paused. He started to whisper. "*Call authorities?* Also, since when do you write poetry?" I was going slow, packing my things. I wanted to talk to Ms. Poss about the poem, so stalling. Someone kicked my desk, right beside my hand, but I won't say who. Doesn't matter. Since it's the last day of school, they go away shortly. (Except for Luca, who stays.)

"Well, call me on Susannah when you get home," Luca said. "Susannah" is what we named my landline. I don't have a cell phone. "I have some news," he said, "I think you'll like to hear."

Ms. Poss had a special bookcase. Ms. Poss was standing in front of the special bookcase when Luca left, finally.

"Thank you for saying that about my poem, Ms. Poss." *But maybe, next time, ask my permission first, before you read it aloud to the whole class.*

"Berryman, Dickinson, Dove," Ms. Poss narrated. "And why not Ginsberg and Myles"—she put a book called *Sorry, Tree* onto the stack, and I loved that title so much I could have cried—"Oh, and Frank

O'Hara! It's summer, after all. Why not have a little fun? And if you're writing about the mother, then you've got to read Sexton—and Plath. So we've got the Plath, and here's the Sexton. And here's Adrienne Rich—you'll like her." A stack of six became a stack of seven, became a stack of eight, became.

A stack of nine.

I stared.

Was it too much?

She wanted to lend them all to me?

"Are you sure, Ms. Poss?"

"Oh, sure. Just bring them all back when school starts." She flicked her hand back over her shoulder. "I really did love the poem, Avery. You have a voice, you have talent."

Pal, my grandpa—and the fisherman from my poem—was waiting for me in the parking lot.

Murky grit on his *I'd Rather Be Fishing* bumper sticker. Truck engine off.

Sometimes if he left the truck engine on, somebody would say something. Always made him feel bad.

He loved trees. Loved water.

(*Gone Fishin'* reads the bulletin)

(one bulletin for each person who pays respects)

(nervous we printed way too many)

(nervous he wasn't loved as much as we feel he deserved)

(as much as he deserved)

Now Pal, as most of you knew him,

actually founded an organization in 2005 called The Great Outdoors, a gathering of progressive outdoor sportsfolk, and we'd gather every month to write our government officials about the dangers of oil, of littering, overfishing certain bodies of water—you name it. We gathered once a month every month for the entire duration of George W's second term.

(he pronounced "W" like Pal always did)

("Dubya")

Now if it offends any of you all that I'm getting a little political here, allow me to speak for our dearly departed—our dear Pal—when I put it bluntly, "I don't care."

(some laughter)

(I look at Mom)

(she smiles)

And while he certainly wasn't perfect—none of us are—

(some nodding)

Pal was as close to a perfect friend as I ever could have asked for.

Local through federal, Pal wrote his officials with concerns about pollution. But sometimes it would slip his mind to turn his truck engine off.

This time the engine wasn't running, but the radio was on. I don't think he realized how on. Tuned to B08.1-The Trolling Motor, *"—always!"* That was the radio station's tagline: *"—always!"* and Pal—short for "Grandpal," the name he gave himself when I was born—was always tuned in.

"Hey, partner! I thought you're supposed to be getting rid of books today, not packing more in!"

Truck window down.

Some people stared. Looking from the truck to me, back to him to me, to the truck.

"Have a nice summer!" I waved to them. I piled into the truck. "It's been real," I tried, and then, "Goodbye!"

And see—just like that, they're gone.

Next, we went to McDonald's. Pal got an extra McFlurry—"what, it's for Babs!" he said. Not true. He would definitely end up eating it himself. Pal hoarded those things like secrets inside his little shop freezer-fridge, and besides, Babs didn't even like sweets. Although, sure enough, last Valentine's Day, the heart-shaped box had come out—*To Babs, Love, Pal*—and what could Babs do but accept it with an eye roll? Pal and I divided the chocolates up and ate them, eventually. Pal could be selfish in this way he had. He wouldn't mean it, but he could be.

"Last-day-of-school! Last-day-of-school!" The people in the drive-through were chanting, and we clapped along.

Next, he dropped me off at my house. "All right, partner!" Then he pulled across the street and parked in his garage. He stood at its mouth and called over to me.

"You get bored and want to come over later, come on! I know Babs'd love to see you."

I was digging my keys out of my backpack, distracted. "Oh okay," I said absently, barely looking up.

I let myself inside.

Took my shoes off in the mudroom.

I stacked the stack of books beside a stack of bills on the kitchen table. The bills were for me, and there was a note too, from Mom—*Ave, Happy last day! Will you enter these bills into QuickBooks for me? Would be a huge help. Love, Mom*—and Susannah was blinking. She had a message on her machine. Beside her, a mason jar sweated. Melting ice with light brown in it. It could have been iced tea, easily, I reasoned.

I pressed the play button—"This message is for Avery Fowell, back in 1973 or some other time when landlines weren't obsolete. Avery, call me when you get a second. I have exciting news. Or you can just come over. Whatever. Byeeee." Luca lived right next door. Made him kind of hard to avoid.

I moved the stack of bills to my desk and the

stack of books to my bed. There was something exciting about the books, seeing them there, on the bed. Sexy even. The way they were just strewn there. The poets. I wanted one to choose me, not for me to have to choose. I decided that for every bill I stuck into QuickBooks, I got one online search of a poet.

Sylvia Plath (1932–1963); notable works *The Colossus*, *The Bell Jar: A Novel*, *Ariel*, the latter published posthumously; famous poems "Tulips," "Daddy," "Lady Lazarus," "Fever 103°"; death by carbon monoxide poisoning, a suicide, put her kids to bed and sealed herself inside her

kitchen & turned on the gas in the oven & opened the door &

Pal cared fiercely for his family, his Kris and his Avery

(okay, okay, now don't *try* to make us cry)

and even after she passed away, it's no secret he kept right on loving Nell

(Nell, Mom's mom)

(no mention of Babs, and Babs is here, I saw her)

and it does me good to think they are reunited now—

(awkward)

(I don't look at Mom)

(because I can't)

John Berryman (1914–1972); notable works *77 Dream Songs*, and *His Toy, His Dream, His Rest*, both later collected in one volume as *The Dream Songs*; famous poems "Dream Song 14," "Dream Song 29," "Dream Song 76 (Henry's Confession)," "The Dispossessed"; death by suicide, threw himself from a bridge, and missed the water;

hearsay is he waved before he jumped

in this next phase of

their journey,

(this guy, Pal's friend, is crying now)

to think they're back together

(it's a heartfelt elegy—I mean eulogy)

after all this time apart,

at the gates of Heaven, her saying, "Pal,
where ya been?"

Anne Sexton (1928–1974); notable works *Live or
Die*, *Transformations*, *The Awful Rowing toward
God*, the latter published posthumously; famous poems
"Suicide Note," "45 Mercy Street," "The Ballad of

the Lonely Masturbator," "Rapunzel"; death by carbon monoxide poisoning, a suicide, hard at work on a
new book, had just been to a meeting with her editor,
took off her rings, poured a glass of vodka, put on her

mother's coat & walked into her garage,
locked herself inside, turned on the car

Mom stuck her head inside my room. I hadn't
heard her come home. "What're all these?" She sat
on my bed. She picked up the Sexton.

If she had picked up the Berryman or the Plath—

"They're books of poems. Ms. Poss loaned them to
me. She read my poem aloud in class today. She said
she thinks I have a lot of talent."

and now Avery, the grandson, is going to

come up here and read us a poem. Aren't

you, Avery?

(yes, that is the plan. it's in the bulletin. why

are you asking me from the pulpit?)

"Awesome." Mom did not open the Sexton. She just
cooled it in her lap.

"I have to drop these graduation cakes off at the
lake club." Life as a professional, self-employed caterer.
"Six total. Can you come with me? I don't want them
to go sliding all over the Volvo."

Did not ask me to drive. Just asked me to ride. So,
she hadn't been drinking—how do I know? Because
she would have asked me to drive. She had asked me
before, when she'd been drinking.

She would have asked me. She would have.

"Yeah, definitely," I said. "Just a second." One more search once she leaves the room.

Frank O'Hara (1926–1966); notable works *Meditations in an Emergency, Lunch Poems, The Collected Poems*, the latter published posthumously; famous poems "The Day Lady Died," "My Heart," "Homosexuality," "Personal Poem"; death by accident, struck by a dune buggy

on a beach on Fire Island & taken to a
hospital where he died, one day later

so at least that wasn't a suicide.

THEN, WHAT HAPPENED WAS

We were driving across town. Six iced cakes. Trying to preserve them in that humidity. All that frosting, gliding. Occasionally some gold crust cresting. It was sunny. All the way to the lake club. One hour round-trip—or eleven hours, when you factored in the hospital.

No air-conditioning inside that beat little beige Volvo either. (RIP, Volvo. Sorry.) Mom, distracted and driving. Me, frustrated, sulking. Thinking about how all those poets died.

The cakes.

The passenger seat.

Tight little Yonah Ave & street parking.

Compadres—

all graduating seniors half off empanadas!

congrats!

As far as stop signs go, poor visibility.

Some shadow from overhanging brush,

obscuring it.

We ran it, in the hot car.

Hit another car.

Or, well, it hit us. But it was our fault.

Door impounded.

Patellar tendon thrashed. Right behind the

knee.

I didn't feel a thing

at first.

"Was she drunk?" Who was asking?

   "No, um, I don't think so."

"Well, how did she seem?"

"She seemed a little tired really, and that was all I noticed." It was Babs asking. "I mean, I realize I'm not a human breathalyzer, but I'm pretty confident."

Babs shook her head.

"You're protecting her."

We were all okay. Everyone. Except for the six cakes. Some icing on the windshield. Looked like a joke. I was home again.

I had a cast, not plaster, but heavy on the padding. "Was she drunk?" *Déjà vu*. Except this time it was Luca who was asking.

"I don't want to tell you. It's nothing personal."

"You don't want to tell me? I'm your best friend in the whole world, and you don't want to tell me?"

He was hurt. But I hurt worse. Which doesn't

mean I was trying to hurt him more. "It's nothing personal," I swore. It's just that he would blab.

And so he got up and left.

When he came back, he was wearing a tank top, gym shorts. I could see his penis outline. A little sunburn on his face. I had lashed out, he explained. But it was fine. I was going through a tough time—he understood. He knew exactly how I felt. He had an alcoholic mom too, in case I didn't recall. He was carrying a new mix CD too, *Feel Better Mix—Songs Sia Wrote But Did Not Record*. Spears, Dion, Perry, and Aguilera—they all figured, as well as a few artists I hadn't heard of.

"You'll like this," Luca said, nudging it against my set knee. "It's high pop."

Our moms' history together: bender buddies, and then best friends. *Gia Abbaticchio+Krissanne Fowell* in a heart shape. Birthed more friendship too, when Luca met me, same age: 7.

We got our toughness from our moms.

And Gia, when she quit drinking, got even tougher. Built a henhouse in their backyard, despite city laws, and harvested their eggs.

Luca got even tougher too. Big, proud muscles from all the protein.

Gia became Mom's AA sponsor, and then it was like Luca became *my* sponsor, got on my nerves sometimes when I felt a little condescended to.

He and I remained and would remain. Steadfast, he assured. He had talked it over with Gia and then gone on a run to decompress. He felt better now. He sat on the edge of the bed, and I looked at his lap.

"I aced Bio," I said finally, and his face lit up.

Our bargain was that if we both aced Bio, we would finally have sex, for our first times each, with each other.

"So did I! That was my news I was trying to tell you on Friday, but you wouldn't leave Ms. Poss's room. . . ."

Luca, as a fourth grader, asked if I could stay his same age when it was my birthday. I thought that was so radical.

". . . I got kind of nervous, like you were . . . unsure or something."

"I can be unsure."

How we compromised: We had his secret birthday, like an elopement. We aged him by a few months to ten, so we'd be ten together. Shit, I was relieved. Ten looked lonely without him.

"I know! I know you can be unsure! That's not what I'm saying, I just . . . I feel comfortable with *you*, and . . . and I love you and . . . you know. You're my best friend."

"You're my best friend too, and I feel comfortable with you." I had to laugh. "Now, the having sex— like having *sex* sex—part is . . ."

"Well, we'll just start at the start, you know? A little mutual jerkage, a little—"

Radical.

There was a knock on the door. "Come in!" Luca called, like he had some authority. It was Mom. "Hi, Kris," Luca went, which I'm sure was annoying. She had a scented candle. Green, palm-sized, palm(tree)-scented candle; when I made the association, between palms, I laughed.

"You are laughing at me. I feel helpless," she said.

"I don't know what else I can say to you now, except I am sorry, and I have already said that."

When she walked out, Luca looked at me, eyebrows raised. I couldn't meet him. I was too bummed out.

He kept talking. "I mean, I guess eventually we'll have to talk about *other* things."

"Like what?"

"Oh, like, you know, we'll have to talk about who wants to bottom and who wants to top."

"Yeah," I said. "At some point."

"Like, do you have a preference?"

"Um." I thought about it. I thought about Mom being somewhere in the house, even though the door was closed.

I was looking at his boner. He started laughing, because we were suddenly so exposed. I shushed him.

I was laughing too, but quietly. It felt surreal to be talking about sex in a *real* way—when it had been jokes, mostly, beforehand. Even the deal, when we struck it, had felt like a joke. Luca picked up the *Feel Better* mix and slid it into the computer drive. The first song—"Pretty Hurts," by Beyoncé—started. "Want me to leave it playing for you?"

"Are you about to leave?"

"Yeah, I think so," he said. "But I'll be back." And I couldn't believe he was just leaving. Like we had just talked about that stuff, and now it appeared we were done, so he was leaving, and it felt a little like abandonment, even though it wasn't—at least not any real kind of abandonment. I knew what the real kind was. But it got on top of me. And in a little while, I started to ache. I couldn't locate it all the way, at first. But it was real and full, like when Sia belts out, *"I'm aliiiive!!"* in that song. Thrilling because, beneath the pain of it, you get the sense there might be something else. Whatever the thing is that pushes. It's urgent and unstoppable, and it holds you. It's the same with masturbating, when you get to that point. And even after, your head's in that quiet place—you've come from the sun, so this must be the ozone—and in that state, it hits you: *I'm alone.* And you think, *If I could just bring this back with me. . . .*

A squirreled dirty pair of gym shorts beneath the mattress. I fell asleep—"Ave?" I woke up. Mom was outside the door.

"I'm going to a meeting in a little while with Gia, okay? I'll be back tonight."

"Okay." I shut my eyes. Sleep again.

I woke to Pal's heavy steps in his rubber-soled boots coming up the hallway, and behind his footsteps, his grunting.

he was always, sort of, grunting

(some people laugh, familiar)

He opened my door and crossed my room and, bless him, I know he was trying to be quiet. He sat at the computer desk. We shared the computer. This was not a violation.

He jiggled the mouse. Began to click a little, type a little, click a little, type a little, clicked some more and typed some more, and then got quiet while scrolling.

I rose up, loud—"Pal!" ("Pow!") Pal jumped.

"Ho—!" ("Ho—," as he said it, was short for "Holy" maybe, but if that's true, then the "Holy" was short for nothing, because Pal never cursed.)

He tried clicking out of whatever webpage he was

on (so frantic). The window kept minimizing, maxi-
mizing. Again and again, at such high speed (I couldn't
begin to tell what he was looking at). When it finally
disappeared, his hand went to his chest. His arm
trembled.

"Partner . . ."

He gasped.

"Mom!" I yelled. "Help!"

But then Pal started laughing, not dying.

"Teach you to ease up on me a bit," he said.

"I'll ease up when you're eighty," I said. "Can't be
too careful when you're eighty."

"You mean I'm not eighty yet? You mean, that
wasn't the birthday we had the stuck pig?"

Now he was joking again. He knew—

"That was your seventy-fifth. Your seventy-fifth
and don't remind me about that pig." *Charlotte*, I

remembered, the pig's name—and it bugged me how they got it wrong, if they were making a *Charlotte's Web* reference. Charlotte was the spider. Wilbur was the pig.

"Why is it so quiet in here? Seems like every time I come in here, there's some music playing."

"There was some playing when I fell asleep. It must have played through, already. Luca dropped off a new mix."

"What's on it?"

"Songs Sia wrote but didn't record."

"She didn't record them?"

"No, she sold them to other artists for them to sing. Like 'Pretty Hurts'—did I ever play that one for you? The Beyoncé song?"

"I don't know."

"Well, here, put the mix in. It's track one."

a thing I got to know about Pal that I feel

lucky to know, that not everyone who knew

him got to know, was that he had a real pop

music sensibility

(some people laughed)

he just had really good taste in pop music

(a few people nodded their heads, knowing,

but they didn't know)

(he subscribed to HBO, so we could all

watch *Lemonade*, for instance)

(how I learned about Warsan Shire, the poet)

(whose work Beyoncé reads in all the

voice-overs)

(woke something inside of me)

"How's the old patellar?"

"It's fine. I've got that good medicine."

"For two more days, then we quit it. That stuff is
strong."

"I hate to mention this, but I peed earlier."

"You peed, huh? You use your thing?"

"I used it, all right. The worst."

I stretched to open the big bottom drawer of
my desk. Inside it, The Alibaba sat capped, a third
filled.

" 'The Alibaba.' Gotta wonder what white person

decided to call it that. I mean, the hero of a classic work of Middle Eastern literature, and they go and name a urine receptacle after him? Why not name the urine receptacle after an American? How about a straight, white, cis, American dude? Name the urine receptacle after him—"

"What classic work did they name it after?"

"'Ali Baba and the Forty Thieves,' you know, from *One Thousand and One Nights*. Like, they could have gone with 'The Gatsby'—I mean, it looks like a cocktail mixer, for crying out loud, a clear cocktail mixer. 'The Gatsby.' That would have been genius!" I was nervous-talking, sort of loud. Embarrassed about having to pee in the container all the time, and Pal having to empty it out, and all.

"Well, it's clear, so the doctors can check real fast and see if you're hydrated . . . I think you're fine, by the way! Ha-ha!"

He looked at me, a corner of his mouth lifting. Something leapt into my throat, jagged like a piece of rubble. I swallowed it back.

"Piece of Doublemint?" Pal asked. He pulled a pack from inside his pocket. "Chew on this, help you get back into rhythm."

"You want to split one?" My hands shook as I unwrapped the foil.

"Nah, you can take a whole."

I ripped it in half just the same. I'd chew the second half later. As I started to smack the first half, Pal instructed, "Go on and chew it slow, now."

"Oh, yeah," I said, like I just forgot.

"Laid up like this, you'll have time to think. Some mornings I just lay there and think of *my* granddaddy, my grandma, my sister, my daddy, my mama, Nell . . . You could watch your whole life in your mind like it was a movie."

Or not. Why would I want to watch that?

Pal took the silver wrapper from the gum and folded it into a silver jighead. He put it on the nightstand beside me.

I smacked on the gum.

"Chew slow, remember?" he said.

Good News &
Bad News

The good news: I really only wanted to read and write all summer anyway.

So, day one in the patellar cast wasn't really even all that bad. Pain meds. A little Emily Dickinson. I was a fan of this band called Sorority Noise, and they put out an EP called *It Kindly Stopped for Me*, which I knew was an Emily Dickinson reference, so she's where I started.

Emily Dickinson (1830–1886); death after death, after death, Emily Dickinson's loved ones kept dying, and after months in bed, Emily died of Bright's disease

virtually unknown & having written 1800 poems in her lifetime

and when I had my fill of reading, I put my headphones in and listened to *It Kindly Stopped for Me*, Sorority Noise, tracks: 1. Either Way, 2. A Will, 3. Fource, 4. XC. Luca introduced me to Sorority Noise, but he has a higher threshold for full-on emo. Emo can really get to me, if I don't parse it out right. It can make me feel really *very* sad—I think because I pay more attention than he does, to the lyrics and stuff.

I want to be a poet for that reason. I've got no interest in writing actual "music" music, but at the same time, I think it's incredible that poetry really is—music.

Or music is poetry. Who's to say, really?

"We passed the School, where Children strove / At Recess—in the Ring— / We passed the Fields of Gazing Grain— / We passed the setting Sun—"

Later, Luca came through the window. I read him some Dickinson. "Mm," he went. So maybe Emily wasn't for him. He pulled a Tupperware container from his backpack: some quinoa and vegetables. "You're my hero," I said. We ate together. We didn't really say much, and I wasn't horny so I did not mention Bio again. I did ask Luca to check on the computer for me, under the History tab, to see what Pal had been looking at earlier.

He made a joke about seeing what kind of porn I was watching. "Oh wait, I wonder if this is it.

" 'The High Tides, Low Tides Retreat, for those seeking relief and recovery from the disease of addiction.' "

There was a video. Sort of like a low-budget movie trailer. Fuzzy, synthy strings+grainy resolution. An older white woman touches the shoulder of a younger black woman. "Because *today* is the day

to make a change!"

White savior (I criticize, a white dude). "Because today is the day.

Is the day.

Is the *day*!"

Luca read aloud from the About page: " 'For those seeking relief and recovery from the disease of addiction, The High Tides, Low Tides Retreat is here.

" 'Our mission is to provide a heaven for those seeking relief and recovery from the disease of addiction, fostered in a culture of interpersonal support and a wireless, communal environment.

" 'High Tides, Low Tides seeks to reinforce the necessity of human connection, as well as rest, meditation, and communion with the natural world.' "

"A 'heaven' or a 'haven'?" I asked.

Luca looked.

"A 'haven.' Did I say 'heaven'?

"I mean, it's a good thing, right, if your mom wants to go to this because it will help her. I mean, it sounds kind of rad, doesn't it? Even badass, honestly; I'd go in a heartbeat."

He was overcompensating because, at this point, I was upset and it was obvious. I had turned my back to the computer screen and to him. I didn't want him to convince me. It was okay.

She had a sponsor. She was going to meetings. She was taking the steps it takes to get better. But *"Remember, it's a marathon, not a sprint!"* Or so the card said.

The card was stuck to our fridge for the longest time, from when Mom first started going to meetings. "Hello, my name is Krissanne, and I'm an alcoholic," as I would imagine. Sometimes reenact.

A man in AA had given her that card, and it was a weird situation from the start, had an airbrush feel. The Tortoise and the Hare with red eyes and bloated heads. A card for alcoholics.

They were seeing each other for a little bit. One morning in the kitchen, he was making breakfast. A cliché: adolescent kid coming into his sexuality *confronts* what is, to him, sexuality—a man wearing boxers and a tank, unencumbered because the only other party in the house (who hasn't seen it) is male.

Those were actually pretty happy times, though. Mom doing better, Gia encouraging, and while this guy was around, it was like she had a way to see the future.

It didn't last.

A week before the car/cake crash: Mom hadn't gone to a meeting in almost a month, and Gia was calling and calling the house and leaving messages on Susannah.

It actually showed me how, in a certain way, Gia was as dependent on Mom as much as Mom was dependent on Gia. We turned out the lights in the house like we were hiding from trick-or-treaters because we'd forgotten to buy candy. I thought it was funny, and suggested maybe we could watch a scary movie. But Mom's mood was sunk.

Gia stopped by the house and knocked. We continued to hide. "Are you sure you don't want to go?" I asked, because the meetings generally did empower Mom. She felt less alone, it seemed. She felt better once she had gone.

"Avery, please don't try to guilt me, okay?"

I wasn't trying to guilt her. That was on her, in her own head. She'd been prepping dishes all day for the Immigrants' Rights Coalition, and something had gone wrong. They had asked if she would donate them for a fund-raising event, and of course Mom had said yes.

I had been at school all day, but when I came

home the kitchen was a total wreck. She had left out a simple ingredient. It had messed up the whole thing, she said. She'd had to make it twice. All day she was back and forth between our kitchen and Pal's, had the ovens in both houses going, and had gotten so overwhelmed she found herself crying, she told me. Then she had gone to lie in the bed for a little while, when Babs called to report that the dish inside their oven was burning. Mom had shot back, "Well, take it out, then!" and rather than get up and walk over to Pal's house to inspect the burning dish, she pulled the quilt up over her head and lay in bed for another hour.

It had cost a lot for her to make those dishes, for which she would make nothing.

And though she had wanted to do it, it's like at the end of the day all she could see was the waste.

Mom cooked with liquor sometimes, so it was still around. I think she went for it. *"Remember, it's a marathon, not a sprint!"* Gia banged on the door. We waited it out. She wouldn't go. She was drunk. The last time it happened, before this time, I'd been instructed to tattle on her. The last time it happened, before this time, she had yanked the top tray of the dishwasher off its track and then fallen against the counter.

It had scared me. I'd called Pal. He and Mom had had a long talk, and Babs sat in my room with me. We ate Domino's. When Mom came in later, once they were gone, she asked how my pizza was, and I said it was good. She sat at the edge of my bed. "Avery, I really am—" She shook her head. "Sick."

We had a conversation about how she was really going to commit to getting better, avoiding triggers like stress and self-neglect, and how she would exercise, how she would read, how she would take time to cook "for the love of it" every once in a while, to remember why she loved cooking in the first place, for the experimentation of it, and how maybe she would journal, or start a blog, or make collages out of cutouts from magazines, which she loved doing as a kid, and how she would try not to miss an AA meeting again. And the whole time I couldn't keep from looking at her earrings, shaped like tiny leaves, each with an emerald, her birthstone, nestled into them.

I was thinking about how we might be trapped, my family. And how maybe I didn't believe in recovery, after all. How Pal originally had bought those earrings for Babs, but how he'd gotten the wrong stone, not Babs's amethyst but Mom's emerald. I've read somewhere that emeralds have the power to protect, but did they? How much could they stand?

"Let's get a Top 25 check," Luca said, to cheer me up: "Oh oh, coming in hot, it's 'Green Light' by

Lorde! About to breach the Top 10, so let's see, how many listens? 89! 89 listens to 'Formation' too, but that's probably stalled out. You've moved on—only to come back to it, some day, of course. Let's see, do we have any dark horses encroaching? Hmm . . . hmm . . . okay, Perfume Genius is up a few slots, but no surprise—he's good to study to. Call me crazy, but is 'Cranes in the Sky' up a couple notches from before?"

"It might be," I said. "I put it on loop to help me sleep one night, and I think it played the night through."

"Yeah, it's in the ninth slot now, so—

" 'XC' in the Top 10 now, so." "What's that one again?" "That's the

soft Sorority Noise one that kind of builds." "Oh yeah, oh yeah, those lyrics." "See, here is my breakdown of you, Avery. It's all here."

He points to the song "Heartbeats" by The Knife. "You've got The Knife's version of 'Heartbeats' securely in the Top 5 with 111 listens. Meanwhile, you've got the José González version bringing up the rear of the Top 25, with 63 listens—that's just *it* to me, Ave, and there is absolutely nothing wrong with it. It's just something I notice; in your heart of hearts, you're a big-production pop music guy. You'll choose the pop song every time." He double-clicked "XC" and we listened—"I mean, I *love* this song, Luc," I said. "*Love.* I'm

just not exactly sure
you're correct. Softer
songs are great—"
          "Yeah, but you
          don't exactly
          give them
          repeat listens—
          I guess that's
          all I'm saying,
          and again, I
          don't believe
          there's any-
          thing wrong
          with it." He
          clicks
          "Heartbeats"
          by José
          González. It

really is a pretty cover of the song, but now I'm teasing him because he's giving me a hard time about how I like pop music, like pop music makes me simple or something, when pop music is the greatest because it helps you not only process the most complicated emotions, but dance to them—even *with* them— as well.

I snaked my hand over to the mouse. I was going to try to click The Knife's version. Luca grabbed my hand, and then we were wrestling, to the extent that we could wrestle. Him on the bed, his legs around my waist, me in my cast.

He had my hand trapped, so I tried to use the other. He squeezed my hips. "Easy, easy," I said.

"You are so hot, Avery

       Fowell." He kissed

       me.

Pal had me make him a playlist once. That's like a collection of songs.

(it's an older crowd, by and large, which is why I explain)

He loves Beyoncé

(awkward slip)

(the present tense)

loved

(even more awkward)

I notice headlights from Gia's car pulling in, to drop Mom off.

"Do you need to go?"

"Nah, Mom will just assume I'm over here with you."

"No, I mean, sorry, Luca, but I think you should go because Mom might need to come talk to me or something. Like, it might be better if you're not here."

"Oh, I've got you. I understand, of course." He left like he came. Through the window.

Down the hallway, the shower came on. I was surprised she didn't come talk to me immediately. At least to bring me my pain meds, which were somewhere. In the kitchen maybe? But maybe she thought, because my light was off, I was asleep.

I wouldn't call out for her. I decided this could be

a hurt I could use later in life, on a beach, somewhere. Maybe a retreat. If she didn't bring me the pain meds from the kitchen. The

time my mom, an alcoholic, crashed our car and injured me. Forgot to bring my pain meds, how I lay awake all night hurting.

The bad news: I lay awake all night hurting. Someone knocking on the door, next morning—"Ave, are you decent?" It was Luca. He was joking.

"Yeah."

When he opened the door and walked in, his mouth fell open. "Ave, you don't look good. Are you okay?"

"Pain pill."

He ran to go get it.

"Mom!" He was calling out. For Gia. For his mom, not mine. He got the pain pill. When he came back in and I took the pill and drank water, he started rubbing my shoulders.

"You're here," he said, "you're right here," as though he were tugging me back from somewhere. They had brought me a wheelchair. Gia borrowed it from their church. No deadline to return it, but like the books of poems, it would have to be returned, eventually.

It had a note tied to the arm: *Get better soon*, probably left for a previous user.

Luca helped me get in, to stretch my leg out. Gia was making breakfast in the kitchen. Mom was awake now. "Gia, please. You're helping too much."

"Oh hush, you know those hens make eggs faster than we can eat them. Get a cup of coffee, sit down."

Luca pushed me by her. "Morning, Mom," I said.

"Morning, Kris."

"Oh good, Saint Luca's here too—it's a party! Say, how about we cut the charity act short for the moment, y'all, and just leave your donations in the offering plate on the way out."

Mom always had a barb ready.

Gia cracked an egg against the frying pan
and a deep yellow
yolk slid out. "Bye," she said. We were
ungrateful. Luca
whispered, "I had better go too," and he
followed her out.

Mom grabbed a wooden spoon and stirred. Then she cracked another egg. The eggs were small and brown with dark freckles. She cracked another. It didn't make any sense. Everyone was leaving. Who was eating?

I saw Gia on the sidewalk through the kitchen window, speaking to Luca. He turned back to look at me, through the window.

I knew what was happening. A tattling.

Gia crossed the street to Pal and Babs's house. Babs answered the door and folded her arms. They stood there talking a while.

"Pal!" Babs called. I saw the shape of her mouth. ("Pow!") It wouldn't end well. I pushed, wheels forward. Rode across the linoleum. "Bye." I mimicked Gia. Mom broke ice from the ice tray into a glass and pretended she didn't hear me. A knock came to the door; she wouldn't hear that either. Turned on the garbage disposal. Pal was knocking. She knew and I knew, and she wouldn't hear it.

"Kris! Kris! Open this door!"

Meanwhile, at the bathroom door, I was thinking, *I got this.*

Pal broke through the screen door of the back porch: The back door was unlocked, so that's how he got inside. He whisked past the bathroom door and didn't see me. In the kitchen Mom slammed the door to the dishwasher, which she one time, drunk, fell into:

> Afterward, tiny injury marks had dotted her legs—"Get out, Dad."

> "Krissanne, what is going on?"

> "You literally <u>broke</u> into my house, Dad, oh my God. Look at my screen!"

"Krissanne, you cannot do this
anymore!"
"Oh, glass houses, Dad!"
Because Pal used to be a drinker too.
("used to be," "a drinker")
Especially in the days after my grand-
mother died.
It had gotten to be a problem.

Mom marched past the bathroom and didn't see me.
When Pal followed her: He saw me.

I had toppled the wheelchair by accident to a
slant against the sink, and it jammed inside
the doorway. "Partner, what happened?" I
hadn't peed myself, so that was lucky, but it

embarrassed me how he lifted me. Like I was
a kid, setting me on the toilet seat: degrading:

so that I couldn't be grateful, could only be
hurt. (Sorry, Pal.) I asked him to
        leave. He kicked the wheelchair. "Piece
        of crap."

                "It was my fault," I
                said, "not the chair's."
                Meanwhile Mom was
                calling out for us. She
                walked right past the
                bathroom again—

"Where did you *go*?"

    "We're in here," Pal called. "Just a minute!" But
she stepped inside the doorway anyway.

"Mom, please! Some privacy!"

And so then she and I were shouting, and meanwhile I was on the commode, not because I was using it, but because I couldn't get up. "You-do-not-tell-me-what-to-do." She clapped it out. It had the same cadence as when you read *Green Eggs and Ham*. It morphed into something like a pep rally chant: "I am the mother, I am the mother, I am the mother." And it worked in the way some sad stories work, if I tell them from far enough away. I can distort them and accent the absurd. I can spin them sort of funny. So I took myself out of it, enough that I could see it, see it more than feel it, to make it funny. So I could laugh at her, right in her face. The sharpest tool I had. The cruelest thing I knew to do. She was already behind me—I was exiting the scene. For a moment I had known her better. How to hurt her worse than she could anticipate. It was the line at the end of the prayer where the pastor rumbles, "Lord, if we love You, let us cry out—" and the whole congregation applauds, "—*amen!*"

It was a lot like last time. Babs brought over dinner for us, which she and I ate in my room, while Mom and Pal had a serious talk in the kitchen. Babs brought a meat-heavy Southern meal this time, so I was only eating potato salad. "You need protein, Avery. You *need* meat." But we didn't eat meat, neither Mom nor I, and Babs knew that. End of story. Then she started in on The High Tides, Low Tides Retreat:

"You know, it gets its name from a Bob Marley song. They believe in spending time outdoors, no phones. It sounds exactly like the kind of thing she will love, which doesn't mean it's cheap, unfortunately, but . . ."

Babs had canceled a cruise, she told me, so that I could come live with them while Mom was gone: just for a month or so . . . I was tuning her out, to a song Sia wrote but didn't record.

"We'll put you up inside the garden room" . . . "Shine bright like a diamond," I was humming . . . "Shine bright like a—"

"Want me to put some music on for you, Avery?" She

put her hand on my
shoulder. Like we
were on that beach at
The High Tides, Low
Tides Retreat: that
video: pixels & sand: water & sun: &
people: all white, white so terribly: big font & bad
sky.

1.

Today

is the day!

Grainy: sad:

THE GOODBYE

2.

I pull on dress   beads

    some bracelets   she never wore

and scarf   I one time   will wear to

    one art school   or another &

    I will put on heels   some rouge

well   maybe   no rouge.

Wait a second.

This is not my   gay fairy-tale.

This bathroom is   bare!

Who will I be   today   when she left me

        so practically

NOTHING

to

work with!

That day, we checked our horoscopes for the month
of June. Mom's said hers was a bad month for

travel; mine said it was a good month to make friends. We both laughed.

On the front lawn: saying goodbye, she nearly toppled me, hugging me. I was propped up by crutches. *This is traumatic for both of us*, I thought. "Kris, be careful," Pal said, and I wished he hadn't. It was fine. Why put it in her head that she can't even say goodbye right?

When they were gone I lowered myself into the flowerbed. Babs sat next to me. The pine straw between us dead enough to be ash.

"Has she ever flown before? Mom?

"Much less by herself?"

"She will be fine, sweet Avery," Babs said. "I promise.

"I changed the sheets inside the garden room. Best room in the house, and believe me I know. It's the only one you can't hear Pal snoring from."

But I hated the garden room. It was dank and always dark, and it creeped me out, and it smelled bad.

I said thanks, anyway.

3.

Oh this one is   more like it

Chanel No. 5   oh yes, oh please

and flower   petals   to dry my

eyes,   oh   flowers,

you are

FAKE!

Tell me:

in whose synthetic

felt

cloth

dream

DO YOU BELONG?

THE GARDEN ROOM, OR "CARBON, NOT MONOXIDE, POISONING"

4.

In order to aid in prolonging the life spans of: copper plants, dead nettle, yesterday-today-and-tomorrow plants, &c.,

I must keep the shade drawn in the garden room for every 2.5hr/3.

Every three hours in the garden room, I was allowed to un-draw the heavy terry-cloth shade, purple. For only one half hour. It took me a while, but I got the gist.

I had a book light.

"No one's making you stay cooped up in here, partner," Pal said. Oh okay, so maybe it was a tactic! Maybe they were trying to smoke me out of there or something. Get me walking, exercising my knee. The threat of "carbon, not monoxide, poisoning"—crafty!

"You seem a little agro," Luca said one day. "No offense." But I'd been reading the Plath and the Sexton, so, "I'm just in a weird headspace," I said, "I'm sorry." He had brought me some quinoa and kale and a new mix: *Songs About, But Not Commonly Played At, Weddings*:

Tracks: 1. "Death of an Interior Decorator," Death Cab for Cutie, 2. "Speak Now," Taylor Swift, 3. "Today,"

Joshua Radin, 4. "Wedding Bells," Coldplay, 5. "White Wedding," Billy Idol, 6. "Wedding Song," Yeah Yeah Yeahs

It was short, so I could tell he'd made it in a hurry.

"Thank you, Luca." We didn't kiss. I worried something was off. When Pal came in later, he asked what my book was about— *Ariel* by Plath.

"Well, there is a lot in it about being a mom and being sick with depression and—" I realized I should have just said "hooks" and "tulips"; I tried to recover.

"Honestly, it's mostly about hooks and tulips. That's basically it."

"Plenty of those outside. Hooks in the shop, tulips in the garden. Just right outside—"

5.

"Let's walk to the shop, get some vitamin D."

"I'll do it for you, Pal. Won't do it for me."

"You really think I can make it all the way to the shop?"

"I sure do."

"But it's all the way across the yard! And it's down a hill!"

"You can do it, partner. Just one step at a time."

Babs said, "One . . . Pal, are you helping me?"

"Yes."

"Two."

They were little brick steps.

"Three."

I could have sworn there were only four of them.

But there were actually five.

"Fi—"

I went swinging myself over that last step like it was the ground.

"Partner!"

"Avery!"

(crunch)

      (crunch, crunch)

      (someone chewing a mint in here)

      (who chews a mint at a funeral?)

      I think Pal liked pop music because it was fun to listen to, and it was an escape—Pal went through some dark emotional times as y'all know. He lost his wife to cancer. He had periodic health troubles. Of course he didn't only like pop music. He also liked jazz and blues and soul. He had depth. His favorite musicians were John Coltrane and Thelonious Monk. He loved B.B. King and Elvis. He loved Donny Hathaway. He loved Roberta Flack. He loved music and fishing, and he liked movies. His favorite movies were *The Searchers* and *Rebel Without a Cause*, both of which he showed me when I was fairly young, maybe too young

(people laugh)

and which opened up whole new worlds to me.

His favorite books were *A River Runs Through It* by Norman Maclean and *The Compleat Angler* by Izaak Walton. *The Compleat Angler* was written in the eighteenth century, and is about making the discovery that you're never alone.

A River Runs Through It is about the depth of an individual's love for his family, and all of the complications that come from such a deep love.

Pal loved his family. He loved

(I take a breath)

my mom and me

(breath)

and since I can't sing any of the songs I've mentioned, and since it wouldn't be worth it to summarize any of his favorite movies or books any further, and since I don't know very much about fishing, I'm going to share a poem that Pal showed me.

A scuppernong vine woven on a thin metal wire stretched from the roof of the back porch to the roof of Pal's shop. Make a zip line. Easy. Take a rolling pin, pass it over the top, grip down, drop, roll, and fly.

I asked if I could go back to the pain pill for the night.

Me: "Also, what am I crushing?"

Babs: "Some impatiens."

Me: "I'm sorry."

Pal: "We've got extra-strength Tylenol. You can have that. How's that sound?"

Me: "It sounds great, Pal."

Babs: "Avery, do not be sarcastic with your grandpa. He doesn't get it."

Me: "I'm sorry about your impatiens, Babs."

We were all pumping adrenaline. They picked me up. Set me back in the wheelchair. A sudden shock.

Took my breath away. Pal wheeled me to the garden room. "A tiny extra bit of vitamin D for you anyway, huh?"

He was trying to make peace. He sat down in the metal chair next to the open bag of topsoil. The chair joints squeaked. Blue tarp lining the floor rattled.

"You know, I've been trying to remember this poem I loved, used to love, probably. Would still love, about a fish. But I just can't seem to—"

"Do you remember who wrote it?"

"I can't. I might have to go look it up on the computer."

It's called "The Fish." It was written by the poet Elizabeth Bishop.

(one nod of recognition—Ms. Poss)

Pal loved this poem.

Pal returned later with the poem. He had printed it out.

"Now read this and tell me this ain't a great poem." He set it on the bedside table, beside a fern.

6.

"Your last ibuprofen," Babs said before bed.
"It's bad for your liver." So I dreamed in
several ways about my body failing.

In one dream, I was at the supermarket
and noticed some of the meat there was
my own. I woke up.

7.

Sylvia Plath was in
the room with me. She put a
finger to her lips. Help me,
she said, so I got out of bed.

She offered me a roll of
duct tape. We need to seal the
doors, she said. We don't
want what's in to get out;
what's more, we don't want
what's out to get in!

Why? I asked. What's out
there?

Tulips, she said. Lots of them, and believe me, I know what it's like to be trapped inside a room

filled with tulips. It's dreadful.

The vivid tulips eat my oxygen. I wrote that, you know? I lived it too.

And what's in here that we want to keep in? I asked.

The soul of a poet, she

answered. We have to pro-
tect it.

By now, we had finished
sealing the door.

She took the duct tape
from my hand, and then came
a knock on the door—it was
dreadful.

Sylvia hit the deck.

It's the tulips! she whispered. Get down!

8.

Oooh-ooh-*ohhhh*, went
the tulips outside. Ah-

ahhh-ah-*ahhhh*.

Ha, one tulip went.

You know it sounds
just a little bit like we're
having sex.

The other tulip, a male,
trilled with laughter.

9.

I know those voices,
Sylvia said. I'd know them
anywhere.

Should we let them in?

Oh heavens no.

But then we heard a sharp striking against the garden room door.

And we knew the tulips had a tool. Something that would easily overpower the duct tape.

They were suddenly inside then, and they were walking toward us.

The tool was an oar. A

white lady with brown hair.
A white man with a bushy
gray beard.

Sylvia, we thought you
were going to help us, the
woman said.

Anne Sexton.

The man, I believe he was
John Berryman, huffed.

10.

I brought the oar, Anne
Sexton said, for crying out
loud! This was your idea,

Sylvia. Your idea, and you
abandoned it!

And *us*, John Berryman
said. Lest we forget, you
abandoned *us* too!

John Berryman seemed
very hurt by this.

The thing is, I'm tired of
rowing, he said.

I'm just fucking tired of
rowing.

You and me both, babe,

Anne said. She dropped the
oar and stepped over to him.

The only one missing was
Emily.

Where's Emily? I asked.

Oh where do you *think*
Emily is? Anne spat. God!

I'm keeping an eye on
this poet soul for now, Sylvia
said. So that my own soul
has a purpose.

We had purpose enough,
John roared, *before!*

Oh hush, Johnny boy,
hush.

Anne read, *Once upon a
time there was a poet soul and
it was very loved, and it had
purpose, and it was called by
the name of John Berryman.*

*John Berryman was loved
dearly by all who knew him,
and he continues to be read
and taught to this day.*

John Berryman fell
promptly asleep on her
shoulder.

Anne said, Can we use
this? She pointed to the
bed—So, what all have you
written, poet?

Well, if you go in my
backpack—I gestured. Sylvia
was on it. Sylvia riffled
through and found a copy of
"I'll Never Eat Fish-Eggs . . ."

She showed it to Anne,
while I opened my notebook
to my works in progress.

Anne read.

She looked stern and was
completely silent.

When she looked up,
she said it was brave to be
ruthless toward the mother.

It is brave to be ruthless
toward the mother.

But that's all, really, I can
say, really, for these poems, as
I don't very much care for
them otherwise, if I'm honest.

She passed the poems to
Sylvia. I felt exposed and like
I might start crying.

John Berryman was
snoring.

11.

You're right, Sylvia said,
after having read a few herself.

He is not a great poet. But
then again, neither was I,
really, when I was his age.
Some even say neither was I
when I—

Oh hush, Anne said. You
were a great poet, Sylvia.

Right then, her kindness
made Sylvia cry.

I held out my sleeve.

So how do I become a
great poet then? I asked. Do
I just practice more?

12.

Have a lot of sex! John
Berryman piped up. He was
awake now, but maybe still
half inside a dream.

I laughed, sort of
embarrassed.

He's not wrong, Anne
said. And when I looked at
Sylvia, she was nodding.

Have you ever had sex
before, poet?

No, but I'm sort of plan-
ning to, soon.

With whom?

My best friend.

And what is her name?

His name, I said, is Luca.

13.

Fascinating! Anne lit a
cigarette.

I find sex between men
fascinating. Cigarette, John?

I won't say no.

Have you ever thought
about homo-sexuality in
relation to evolution?

I shook my head.

Good, Anne said. Don't

think about it. No, the key is
to live your life free of the
burden of evolution.

Desire, passion. That's
what's real. That's what feeds
your poetry.

And if you can make
yourself into the smallest
version of yourself, John
added, write that. That will
feed your poetry too.

His eyes were closing. He
was about to doze again.

14.

Now may we use your
bed tonight, poet?

Anne flicked some ash
into a ceramic pot from
which some dead nettle
grew.

We are very tired from all
the constant rowing.

Constant rowing, I
repeated.

And John's advice: If you
can make yourself into the

smallest version of yourself,
write that.

We fell asleep. I dreamt
then about my teeth rotting.
They were like chalk and
my saliva kept dissolving them.

I tried to go to school.
Tried to convince myself it
looked normal.

When I woke up, all the
poets were sleeping facedown,
hands down their fronts.

I didn't know what they

were dreaming: I wanted to
be dreaming it.

Sunday, Babs came in with her Bible and cups of tea. "You know, you are a Job." She opened the Bible. "Because you are facing so much right now, and I'm sure you are just like, 'God, what is going on?' "

The tea had Saint John's Wort in it. I sipped. "I don't honestly feel like that," I said. I actually felt sort of okay, in the moment. I had written a poem that I liked, that interested me. It was under my bedsheet like a heating pad. Babs kissed me on the forehead.

"Oh, there go the Abbaticchios." She nodded at the window. Luca and Gia piling into Gia's yellow sedan. "That's two prayers getting said for your mom today. Well, three, including mine."

I wanted the Abbaticchios to see me. Maybe what I wanted was a prayer, or maybe what I wanted was to be missed. Maybe after noticing the copper plant first, and then me sitting up behind it, the Abbaticchios waving, "Oh look, there's Avery! There's Avery!"

Allen Ginsberg (1926–1997); notable works *Howl and Other Poems*, *Kaddish and Other Poems*, *Mind Breaths*, *White Shroud*; famous poems "Howl," "America," "Sunflower Sutra," "Kaddish"; death, after failing to be treated for congestive heart failure, Ginsberg spent days calling up loved ones to say goodbye,

        & when he died, he
        was surrounded
        by them.

I read *Kaddish and Other Poems* from start to finish, and began it again immediately. I couldn't get over how *this* was poetry, how it was messy and perfect and how that made it everything. It made me antsy, like caffeine; and the lines from "Kaddish," how when Ginsberg learns his mother has died, he brings her words into the poem, her words that she actually spoke: "The key is in the sunlight at the window in the bars the key." I repeated those words again and again like a prayer. A fourth person, potentially. Praying that day for Mom.

Another poem, called "Poem Rocket," was shaped like a penis. I showed it to Luca, who went "Dick in the aiiiiir!" from this song we love, called "Dick in the Air," and I think that's how we both got horny. Studying Bio that day, when we struck our bargain, it was raining. Luca and I'd been back and forth between our houses, cobbling together notes and cards with definitions: *receptor—organ or cell that responds to external stimuli, sends signal to sensory nerve.*

My chest was damp from the rainwater. One day when we were in fifth grade, Luca had suggested our moms were alcoholics. We were learning about alcoholics in school. How if you abuse alcohol while pregnant, it could mess up the baby. Symptoms: drooping eyelids, big nostrils, thin lips, deformity. "Do we have any of these?" We checked. We took our shirts off. My dent in my chest, my *pectus excavatum*, was there, is there still. I was born with it. "Does this count?"

Luca balled his fist and pressed inside the dip in the breastbone: while studying, he pressed the *receptor* card in, definition down. When he pulled it away, some of the words stuck. "Now if you forget, just check inside your shirt." He climbed into bed with me. He was looking for the definition. "I know it's still stuck to you, cheater."

Now, we tipped the fern off the bedside table. It didn't smash, but it spilled soil all across

the blue tarp. We got nervous. We stopped. Later, Babs asked, "What happened here?"

HOMOSEXUALITY, OR "ALL-YOU-CAN-EAT CRAB LEGS"

15.

    (sigh) today I blew

    on a gardenia ~~leaf~~ petal

    until it turned brown

16.

    That summer, to walk down our street was

    to be overcome by a sense of hot, sticky

    dread: Babs in her garden, Pal in his shop,

    radio blasting, the boy with the bird-in chest

    beneath the tree, buried, all too serene.

(How do I tell this story?)

"And if you can make yourself into
the smallest version of yourself, write
that."
                    —J.B.

17.

Where there was first a boy with a bird-in
chest, there is now but a bird-out chest (a
nest) without a boy. And his mother is out
looking for him.

Meanwhile, the nest incubates.

(Try an egg.)

18.

"So, what we have now," said the father to the mother (who'd since vanished), "is a bird-in chest without the body—without the boy, without the bird—so just the nest. And what are these?"

( )   ( )   ( )   ( )   ( )

"Those are eggs," answered the mother (who'd long since gone), answered on a telephone; they were states apart. The agreement: never to have to see the other's face again. Voices were permitted, and certain decisions.

　　　"And what is to be done about the eggs?"

"The grandparents." The mother, long since disappeared, takes a sip from her solitary bottle. They no longer share, she and the father, the bottles.

"My parents are dead," the father said.

That's how it boiled down to the mother. It always seemed to boil down to the mother.

Boiling bottles (sterilizes), long since past, motionless, still frame, taken from the vantage point of the unhatched (the sole survivor, yes; the father ate the others) at its high-chair-level height.

The egg.

It was bad, I knew. I called it "The Egg." I was out-side under the oak tree. Babs was in a flowerbed. "Oh, that's nice! It's nice to see you outside. It's a good tree; nice to sit under." Across the yard Pal's shop with the window open: B08.1-The Trolling Motor blared "—*always!*" and "—*always!*" again. I think it was get-ting Babs's goat. I think she was craving a little quiet.

"I don't know how you get a thing done with that damn radio playing." It was the first time I ever heard her curse. She went inside for a little while. I cracked open *Sorry, Tree*; I had crutched out to the tree and sat under it to read. I couldn't read a book called *Sorry, Tree* inside. Right in the first pages, a queer

love scene, and why had I spent all this time read-ing straight poets? Ms. Poss should have told me right away: Skip to Ginsberg, skip to Myles! I wrote down:

19.

Poetry is queer really, just by nature.

I needed to think about that. I was right: I knew. Poetry's queer, but I wanted to figure out how, why, I knew it to be so. How, in what way, poetry and queerness are productive.

I wanted it to be more than a feeling. (But why, when feeling had always been good enough for me?)

I jotted down a sentence: "I'm living inside today's bright edges." It just came to me, so I let it sit a while. I didn't quite know why I wrote it or what I meant by it. It wasn't a poem, really. But I liked it. I thought it might be about sadness, about hiding from it. On the line beneath it, I wrote, "But I'm happy (and it may not be, whatever, but I'm) just waiting for her to come home." So, today's prayer for Mom, it turned out. I read it in a whisper. I felt good. I hoped she was on a beach, but not getting her shoulder touched in a way that was condescending, and that maybe if she was having a bad time, at least she was looking forward to coming home.

Babs stepped to the edge of the porch. "Pal!" ("Pow!") He didn't hear: He was in his shop: the radio was too loud: "—always!"

"Always! Always!" Babs mimicking the station, "Always!" stomping. She carried an empty ceramic planter in one arm. It shattered against her hip bone while she knocked. "Pal! You have got to turn it down! I just got a call from Mrs. Shivens next door. It's too loud!"

When he opened the door, she asked, "Are you deaf or something?" She almost whispered it. He looked past her to me, under my tree. "I'm sorry," he said.

"So embarrassing," she said.

20.

She stooped to pick up the clay shards from the doorway. But there turned out to be too many of them. So she left them there.

I crutched across the yard to Pal's shop: counted buds on the scuppernong vine: eleven or so, a small crop. "Pal?" On the inside, I heard a bottle clink. That's how I knew he was drinking. As he put it away, inside his mini freezer-fridge—"Partner! Come on in!"

That was a great poem.

(Ms. Poss pats me on the back)

Better than what you normally get at a funeral.

(I laugh)

(otherwise, I'm crying)

(we aren't doing graveside)

He had good taste, didn't he?

I can see where you get it from.

(I keep crying)

(I'm glad that Mom isn't standing next
to me)

(to see this)

(all hitting me)

I wasn't really using the chair anymore, but Pal
wanted to have it just in case. We didn't fold it
up or even put on its brakes. It was just rolling
around back there. Its final buffer, flimsy tailgate,
and we had to return it to Luca's church. Every
time there was a loud kerplunk, I gritted my teeth.

"You okay, partner?"

"Yes," I said.

We were on our way to the Chinese restaurant: Babs, me, and Pal. Friday: seafood night: all-you-can-eat crab legs in the buffet line.

"I am going to have crab legs. What are you going to have, Babs?" Babs hadn't said a word since she broke the ceramic planter. The shards were still there, a little mound of trouble outside Pal's shop. She didn't reply to the question.

"What about you, partner?" I sort of wanted him to stop talking, stop trying to make us talk back. It is hard for me to admit right now that I was angry at him. So much time he spent in his own little world, on vacation from reality. Sometimes I swear he couldn't see us. The reason he bought Babs chocolate on Valentine's Day. The reason he thought I was clueless about his drinking.

The radio being off made the chair's every budge seem loud.

"Chair or crutches, what do you think?"

"I think crutches," I said. Babs gripped my elbow while I steadied. "Well, I hope nobody steals the chair while we're inside," she said, like she was aggravated we'd brought it.

Inside was crowded, and the air was dense, sticky with salt. It made me sweat a little. By the time we got to the table, Babs had ordered our drinks. She ordered waters. Pal asked the waiter if he could have sweet tea with Splenda packets, and the waiter said of course. His name was Christian. He was cute. The whole place smelled like seawater. I felt seasick: I identified that as the feeling. "What can I get you from the buffet, partner?" Pal stood. I didn't want him to call me "partner" in front of

Christian. Christian was cool. Had an earring and glitter eye makeup. I wanted to leave my place at the table, leave my number behind, *if you're single, or open, and if you're bored* . . . I told Pal just some rice would be nice. He said, "A-OK!" He understood I wasn't feeling quite myself. He wouldn't try to convince me. He came back a moment later with white rice in a shallow bowl. I had two forkfuls and felt full. Babs returned with her plate from the buffet: a few small crab legs. "The dregs," she said. "We might have to go stand in shifts." Pal polished off an egg roll. "I can go next." He took a sip from his tea. He hadn't mixed the Splenda in yet. He made a face. It made me laugh. Christian looked over at us and smiled. Babs sucked the broken edge of one thin leg. "I'm just not getting anything." Even when Pal took his shift in line, he only brought back small pieces. "People are poaching the line. It ain't fair." Babs got up, brought back a plate of rice and chicken. She had wontons. She put one on my plate. "Vegetarian." I took a bite. "I think it has crab in it," I said. I set it back on her plate. She rolled her eyes, and when we were leaving, by the register, she put ten dollars in this little clear box with a coin slot and modest pink label:

GAP: Grandparents-As-Parents: A Local Org.

Avery,

(I look up)

(Babs)

(don't know what to say)

Well, can I hug you at least?

(she does)

(she doesn't hang around long)

(too much hurt)

I love you.

(another goodbye)

(too many)

(she leaves, and Ms. Poss keeps talking)

(I try to listen.)

You know I read every single one of
those damn extra-credit responses and . . .
just terrible. I can tell you're all on Twitter,
24/7.

How can you tell?

Because it's like words, words, words,
words, no articles or compound sentences,
just everything smushed together, enough
"abbrevs," as y'all say, to make me hurl.
Trying to say the most in the fewest number of words. That's what it's coming
down to.

Hasn't that always been the goal, though?

(even Ms. Poss had said it)

(to say as much as you can in as few words
as possible)

(is a strength)

Well, your generation has taken it to new
heights.

(Mom, Gia, and Luca find us)

Did you see her?

(they've been hiding Mom from Babs)

I didn't. She must have slipped out.

(it seemed like a better idea to lie)

(walking to our cars now)

GAP, FAP, PAP & MAP

21.

GAP, FAP, PAP & MAP were friends, almost like The Seven Deadly Sins were friends, or Punch & Judy.

This is a story about relationships.

GAP: Grandparent-As-Parent: I wasn't sleeping. Thinking about Babs putting money into the GAP jar. Eating away at me. I had to pee. I was also thinking about how I might like a cell phone after all. That way, I could text Luca. It'd been days.

I made my way down the hallway with the crutches. Peed, imagined a horror movie, a home invasion + 16 y.o. boy on crutches, a cat-and-mouse deal. Someone knocked. I startled, shot pee into the corner of the bathroom.

"Avery?"

"Yeah?"

"Okay?"

"Yeah."

When I walked out, the lamp in the living room was on. A quilt there, on the couch, where Babs had been sleeping.

"Pal snoring?" I asked.

"We've tried everything," she answered. "Flonase, neti pot, Zyppah, Brez strips. He wore a chinstrap for a while. No progress. And the plants, the sage, dead nettles, then thyme—all snoring remedies, and not a single one worked."

22.

See, GAP was supposed to look after MAP, while PAP was away (at rehab), but the GAP started to undergo meiosis. It's animal, natural, no one's to blame. But MAP was disrupting "the natural flow," as they say:

so MAP went to FAP's house, to see if he wanted to "fap," as they say.

MAP needed touch.

FAP: Friend-As-Parent: "Hey hey, it's been a while!"

I said. "Just a few days," Luca said. "What are you doing?"

"I am . . . I am going to stay at my place for the night. Babs can't sleep very well right now, so she needs the garden room, and I need space. I think they need space from me too. And I can pretty much get around on my own now, so do you want to come hang tonight, maybe watch a movie or something?"

"I've been trying to figure out how to say this to you, Avery, but honestly it's like, I'm sorry, things are a little confusing for me right now. Like I maybe think things are moving too fast, or something,

like maybe I think I need some space."

"You made me a fucking wedding CD!"

23.

But then FAP needed space; it's okay. Even plants need space. MAP understood. He unfolded the map from his pocket. He followed the directions home.

PAP: <u>Parent-As-Parent</u>: Once when I was a kid, I was very sick. I was an allergic kid, got a sinus infection that moved into my chest, coughed for days, probably drove Mom crazy. Probably she got drunk so she could sleep. I remember I got up, walked to the living room. Mom was blacked out on the couch. I tapped her leg. She didn't move. I really couldn't tell if she was alive. I went to the kitchen. I got a cup of water. I came back. I let it drip on her. With every drop, her hand would flinch. It's how I could tell, finally.

I got the medicine myself. I got the cream to rub

on my chest. I got my own glass of water, and I crawled into bed.

24.

      PAP, let's face it, had been unready to be
PAP. It's like when you halt meiosis, it just
doesn't do. No one's to blame.
            Even plants experience it, exactly the
same.

<u>MAP</u>: <u>Myself-As-Parent</u>: I got some eggs from the fridge, light brown with brown freckles. I cracked them into a bowl. I decided I wasn't hungry. I hadn't stirred the yolks together yet. I put the bowl back in the fridge. Opened up the Sexton, read a line I'd

underlined, from "The Gold Key": She introduces a sixteen-year-old boy, who she says is "each of us." No, he's me. I set it down. I stirred the eggs. I poured a glass of vodka. It was in the freezer. Blah, gross. I added ice. I added a splash from some orange power drink. I drank. I swished the eggs around the frying pan. Yolk-swirl. Saw strands of gold hair like Rapunzel, how I could tell I'd been reading the Sexton—or getting drunk—or both.

"Have you ever thought about homo-
sexuality in relation to evolution?"
—A.S.

I watched a video, a science talk about homosexuality and evolution. The scientist was not gay, but his son was. Possessed a "male-loving gene." The scientist said, "There are not that many studies about lesbians, so forgive me." He said,

"The 'male-loving gene' predisposes an infant to being more 'family-centric.' It makes the male more passive as he grows into, not the warrior—not the hunter, not the gatherer—but have you ever heard the term 'gay uncle'?"

Some people laughed.

The good gay uncle. His purpose is to hold the family together.

MAP's purpose, then: to hold everyone together.

"Now, we've also noticed," the scientist continued, "a very strong correlation between men who were born homosexual and mothers who experienced highly stressful pregnancies.

"Like the mom's body has said to her baby, 'Okay, I might not make it out of this. I might need you to be the one to stick around, to look after everyone, in case I am gone,' and then her body flips the switch; it turns the gay genes on."

I stopped the video, and kept drinking. I put on a Sia music video instead, for "Big Girls Cry"—I love how Maddie Ziegler dances in that video. With just her hands and face. Her expressions: mouth gaping, looking stunned. She's afraid. She is angry. She is fighting to live. She is making a hook with her hand, finger crooked inside her mouth. She is biting her wrist. "Sorry," she is mouthing to someone offscreen. It's poetry. Pure poetry. I watched it again, and kept drinking.

25.

MAP has an oar. He is rowing. God, it is an awful rowing. He is following directions.

"I might be in trouble," her body had said. Her mother had died. She was grieving. And she was doing this, by and large, alone. "I might be in trouble." Had I been, then, her prayer?

She used to sing him this hymn for a lullaby: "You are my saving grace / My lighthouse in the storm / You are my rock of a-ages / Whenever I'm forlorn / You are my saving grace—"

She always ended on the first line.

His first exposure to enjambment.

But it was also a hymn. The "you" was God. What does that do to a kid?

Sometimes she would sing it to him over and over again.

He is too tired to write any more poems, read any more poems, tonight. Too noisy. He tries to tune it out with drink. And yet, it's everywhere he looks. Everywhere poetry. He walks out into the street, beneath the streetlamp, and stands. The street spins, a-sudden. He wants to lie down.

He stumbles past bushes in the cool night air. There's a light behind this window. He curls beneath it, a little match girl.

A fairy-tale Anne Sexton never retold.

Except that she did.

She is telling it right now.

Most of the fairy-tales she tells end in bite.

This one ends in love:

A cat happens up to hear the fairy-tale retold. A stray, long-haired tabby with an ancient quality. Her name is Grimalkin, like in a fairy-tale.

The poet Anne Sexton, noticing she has an audience now, restarts the telling. She animates a little. She breezes through her beginning: "The little match girl has had too much to drink tonight, yes, so we will have to light the matches *for* her. So I've brought the matches with me. You'll see there are four, just like in the fairy-tale, and you'll recall—this is canon—that each time the little match girl strikes a match, she sees a vision in the flame. These visions are depictions of happy times, some of which the little match girl has experienced, and some of which she has only imagined: a lighted Christmas tree, a reanimated roasted goose—disturbing if you ask me—"

"Excuse me."

"The goose, it practically jumps out at her—"

"Um, pardon?"

"Yes, cat?"

"Before we go any further, may I ask you why the little match girl has been drinking tonight?"

In response, Anne's eyes roll upward, her open mouth chortles. "Of course she's been drinking, cat— she's an artist, isn't she? Well, a poet, specifically—a particularly torturous trade. We have been known to imbibe!" But then Anne's eyes grow sad, and in a moment of clarity (it would seem), she goes, "I think there are several reasons why our little match girl has been drinking tonight. I think, to look at it simply, she is young and curious. But—to go deeper with it, I think she wants to understand it better, the power of it, how it got such a hold of the people she loves. She wants to confront her fear of it." This is starting to feel like too nice a ribboning. With her thumb, Anne rolls the four matches in her palm. She looks down at them. She wants to end this tale in love.

"Or maybe she feels like it's her turn to have a problem—her turn to make someone worry about *her*, for a change. Maybe she's doing it to teach them a lesson, to demonstrate their power to hurt her, to show that they have hurt her—or otherwise, maybe she just feels doomed to it." Anne looks up. "Or maybe she figures, *hey, I gotta die some way*—I really don't know, cat."

The poet's eyes grow dark.

She slowly brandishes the four matches clutched inside her fist. "So we'll strike the first for her—let's see. My, how the bulb from the strike 'swelled'— how *phallic*—into a vision of . . . let's see: 'The first match lit, and in it, she saw her grandmother. Her grandmother, who died before the little match girl was born—beckoning her, standing over—why, it's a barbecue grill! How funny!" Anne is delighted, restarts, orates accordingly: " 'The first match lit, and in it, she saw her grandmother. Her grandmother, who had died before she was born—beckoning her, arms open, standing over a barbecue grill. In one hand, the grandmother possessed tongs—shining tongs with which she turned cobs of corn wrapped in gleaming silver foil. *Mmm,* thought the little match girl, *then it must be the Fourth of July*—"

"But wait, if you'll please," Grimalkin interrupts softly, "once more-*hrr* . . ." (A mew slipping out, surprising the cat—what happens when she gets emotional.) "How does it end?"

Anne pauses and pulls in a deep breath. She spits the air up against the back of her teeth. *It is very disrespectful to ask a storyteller to reveal her ending*, Anne thinks. Besides, she doesn't know yet how she will end it. *Who does this cat think she is?* Anne wonders. And then she realizes. How she will achieve her ending. How she will end this tale in love.

"I'm afraid you'll have to wait and see, Grimalkin," Anne answers. She looks toward the sky, spreads her arms out, wing-like, and spins. (She must play the comic villain here, the ignoramus, to achieve the ending she wants.)

"In the original telling of the fairy-tale, the little match girl *burns through* all her matches. And in the end, she *freezes*. She *dies*. She dies *alone*!" Anne keeps spinning. She just has to keep rambling like this. Long enough for Grimalkin to get away.

"But perhaps, in *my* retelling, the little match girl will get to die with witnesses! It would be so much *less* depressing that way, don't you think? So much sadder to die alone, would you agree? Wouldn't that indeed be almost happy? If the little match girl got the chance to die with witnesses—her witnesses being you and I, cat?" Anne stops spinning. She lowers her arms, and finally her chin.

She hopes it has worked.

The streetlamps, the dim houses, the cars parked on the road, and the passed-out little match girl on the lawn—each one holds its pose. But the long-haired Grimalkin is missing. Having sauntered over to the house across the street; having perched outside a window of the old couple's house; having begun to yowl and yowl for help (as hoped); she has begun to save the little match girl.

She will yowl—nearly howl—until a light comes on inside the old couple's house, and someone will step outside to shoo her—Babs; who will spot the little match girl—and run to him. That is how the fairy-tale ends. In love.

TO TURN YOUR INSIDE—
RIGHT SIDE—UP AGAIN

The accusation that hurled us into the next morning, the morning after the dull orange drink incident: "It's not just the drinking, Pal—it is the lying, it is the hiding, it is the deceit . . ." Babs pointed it all out. The smuggled sweets he kept hidden—things like ordering two McFlurries on the last day of school, saying one was for her, when I knew he was only going to eat it later, the box of chocolates on Valentine's Day—saying he hadn't been "much of a drinker" since that dark period after Nell died.

"And he has inherited it from *you*! It's in his

genes! He will *always* be trying to get out from under this, Pal!"

("—*always!*")

So we were trapped—at least I was. I hung my head inside the toilet bowl. I could still hear Babs talking. It felt like she was having this great epiphany—"It all started with *you*!"—and the only logical solution—in retrospect, I realize—would be for her to leave.

The full weight of our family had hit her. It had sunken in. I know she was panicked. I know she was worried about me. But maybe now it all seemed bigger—too big. I would always be trying to get out from under it, maybe. But she wouldn't be—she didn't have to be. Is this when she decided to leave us? I can't really say. I will not talk about Babs, I will not talk about Babs, I will not talk about Babs. It is not my place to talk about Babs—to try to tell her story.

But I do have to tell the next scene. That guy who

liked Mom, who gave her that card, and would stand in his underwear—he started to think I was "off" because I wasn't showing an interest in girls. I only wanted to hang out with Luca. He gave Mom these books, fanatical books on guiding cis, hetero, Christian boys through puberty. One was called *Does God Love Gays?* On the title page was the question; on the page right behind it was the answer: *YES—God did love gays!* "And, as a Christian, you should too!" it said. "But remember, Christians are called by God to speak out *vehemently* against sin! So how do we navigate this? This book will tell you."

I found it in a stack of his things, after he was gone. I wasn't sure Mom had seen it. I will not talk about this man, I will not talk about this man, I will not talk about this man who plugged his need to drink with religion, and encouraged my mom to do the same, who made my mom feel happy for a while, but who gave her this book that made her think she did not love me. I will not talk about church, I will not talk about church, I will not talk about church, because I know it is complicated. I know church does a lot of good for a lot of people. I know not every believer is like that man.

So I've cut up the next scene, which is set in a church. I have kept in the good parts, the good advice I was given, which has helped me, and the rest I have weeded out. In those spaces I've included substitutions.

I am still working. On this part especially.

Babs and I waited on sofas in the waiting room. Pal was at home. All morning, after the fight, they hadn't been able to look at each other. He hadn't been able to look at me.

"Avery, you can go on in!" It was the sweet lady at the front desk. She had white hair with bangs and round glasses.

"The pastor is ready for you!"

I crutched in—I'd been feeling like I was over the crutches, almost completely. But I must have banged the patellar in the night because it was sore. Pastor Daisy remarked, "Ah! I could hear you coming—from a mile away—on those Mechanical Wings!"

She had bright red hair, which was tied in a bun, and amplified by the halo through which I was seeing everything: effect of a hangover. That, and a rotten-feeling gut, apparently. She wore the reverend collar and a white coat. "I'm afraid I'm in a bit of a state," she said. "I was gone for two weeks on vacation and left only one instruction, for someone to water my abiah root"—she nodded at the doorway—"and no one did, so . . ."

She pushed her desk chair back and stood. "Do you think you might be willing to lend a hand?"

I followed her out of the office and down the hallway—through the corner of my eye, glimpsed Babs in the waiting room.

Babs was reading a magazine. I didn't think she had brought the magazine on her own, but I also wasn't sure where she had found one. I hadn't noticed any magazines in the waiting room when we were sitting. Maybe she had brought her own but had kept it hidden from me, as though it might offend me. That she might, for a moment in the waiting room, try to escape this. The sunlight coming through the windows, reflecting off the pages—through the halo of the hangover, effect was like vapor. Like light and shadow at the same time. She raised a tissue to her nose, like she had been crying.

I'd never felt so responsible for someone's hurt before. I felt so guilty.

"*Psst*, Avery—" Pastor Daisy was at the back door, the abiah root pot lodged against her hip. "Come on. I don't want to let all the cool air out."

I followed Pastor Daisy outside into a courtyard with a brick path. A fountain, some benches, some trellises with vines. The sunlight blurred every edge. Every object had a soul looming out from its margins. I had to squint my eyes.

"We have these really—really—*lovely* plants back here! Just right beyond the daphne!—called 'ecstatic puff-ball'—have you heard of them?"

"I haven't," I said. "I don't really know plants that well."

"Well, then you'll be—pleased—you see. The

puff-ball is quite *animal*, really." We paused next to a bed of dark soil, from which the puff-balls sprouted like soft white pinecones from their bed.

"See, they look sentient, don't they?" Pastor Daisy lowered the pot. "They're like cannibals—*ah!*" She nudged the clay pot with her heel, and the abiah root whistled out. After two weeks of no watering, it was practically powder. We stood there watching.

"What happens next?"

"The puff-ball overtakes it—it begins to ingest it. See, the 'ecstatic puff-ball' feeds on decay."

"And that happens . . . now?"

"It is happening now, yes."

"And we'll see it?"

"See—what?"

"It ingest?"

"Oh—no, that takes a while. Really, the process is its own sort of decay. But it's fascinating. Shh!—be very quiet, and you'll hear it." She dropped her voice to a whisper. "Do you hear—it—can you hear—it—the *chewing?*" She made a delighted and repulsed noise.

"I can't hear it."

I was jealous.

"Well, after all," she said, "you're only sixteen."

"See—if it really was, as you say it was—a 'one-time deal,' Avery, I'm not too concerned.

"It's just that—you absolutely know what a slippery slope drinking as a means of coping is."

There were two books on her desk: one called *Called Back* and the other called *Are We Almost*

There? They were a bit conservative for her taste, she said.

Then she pulled out some old *Guideposts for Kids* that told "true" stories of children in peril.

"And in this story"—she showed me—"an angel saves a little girl from getting hacked to death by an axe murderer!"

"First it's a drink here, a drink there. Because you're sad, or you're stressed, maybe, occasionally—but then something big happens:

"You know, you lose a parent, God forbid, or a friend.

"You find you have then, well—not to sugarcoat

it—a whole slew of bad days, right in a row, one after the other.

"And so, we have the choice, you know—we make a decision. Do I disappear? It sounds tempting. Or do I make it a practice to stay present, you know?

"Talk to people, talk to God, listen for God—

"Your grandmother—"

"She's not my grandmother."

"Oh, okay."

"Not technically."

"Well, she tells me you're a writer."

"Yeah."

"That makes it hard.

"Hearing voices all the time."

"Voices?"

"Well, in the sense that when you read something, you take in a voice. When you write something, you produce a voice. Voices in, voices out—I deliver a sermon every week. I write constantly. It's exhausting. Even when I'm writing a sermon!—sometimes it's hard to remember that God is like—within me.

"Just like God is within you.

"It's like, from the moment we are born, our first

thought is—'Okay, everything is *out* there, so I have to go get it,' you know?

"My mom is out there, and she has food, and I need food to survive, et cetera, et cetera—

"But when it comes to God, Avery—and listening—you have to plant both of your feet on the floor—"

She stomped her black shoes out from behind her desk.

"You have to be present. You have to be alive!"

But what about remembering? Was there God in memory too? I didn't ask—I didn't even really know to wonder yet.

The placard on her desk said *Pastor Daisy*, but it was sort of a fake placard, made from construction paper, Magic Marker, and glitter. I think a child must have made it.

She had a poster of Mount Vesuvius on her wall.

I asked her if she or anyone she loved had ever struggled with addiction issues. "Oh, sweetheart," she replied. "That's all of us."

On her desk beside her computer, there was a stack of envelopes, many of them halved, and other scraps of paper. I asked if I could borrow a scrap to leave her a note.

She seemed begrudging, like she needed all of them. I said I didn't have to, it was fine. "Oh, just go for it," she said. And that's when I left her a small poem:

"I'm living inside today's bright edges / God, supposedly, lives there too / Sometimes God manspreads, and I complain / I say, 'I only want to learn to love you.'"

After the church visit, Babs and I went to a crowded bookstore. Nobody was in the poetry section. A good selection, though: Anne and Sylvia and John, Eileen, and Allen. I saw Rita Dove, who I was starting next, her book called *Mother Love.*

When a bookseller walked over with a stack of new books, and I asked if she had any recommendations for books by contemporary queer poets, she nearly dropped her stack.

"Literally, it's like I've been waiting my whole life for someone to ask me that."

A stack of seven became a stack of eight. Became a stack of nine, easily.

Babs came over. "Find anything?"

"Um—" The answer was yes. She
saw the stack. *Crush* by Richard
Siken, *The New Testament* by Jericho Brown,
Night Sky with Exit Wounds by Ocean
Vuong, *The Devastation* by Melissa Buzzeo,
[Insert] Boy by Danez Smith, *Useless
Landscape, or A Guide for Boys* by D. A.
Powell, *Autobiography of Red* by Anne
Carson, *Catalog of Unabashed Gratitude* by
Ross Gay, and *Winners Have Yet to Be
Announced: A Song for Donny Hathaway* by
Ed Pavlic—I thought Pal might like that one,
since he liked Donny Hathaway.

"Oh, just get them all," Babs said, and she bought
them for me.

($159.32)

In the car, she started crying. "Let's just take them back to the store, Babs. I'm sure they'll let us return them." She said she wanted me to have them; it was important to her, "because I love you, Avery."

"I love you too, Babs," I said.

When we got home, Pal asked, "What happened? Everything okay?" I went outside and sat underneath my tree and wrote what was mostly plot summary for the end of the egg poems.

26.

After the appointment at the church, the egg
returns to the tree behind its grandparents'
house. The tree has been struck by lightning,
and now the poems are all spelled backward.

( )   ( )   ( )   ( )   ( )   ( )

The egg cries at the death, a little, of its
poetry.

The tree groans. The egg knows. The trunk
sags forward from the root. "The roots
aren't good," the egg observes.

The egg is not on a slope, and so can't roll away quite accurately.

The trunk groans. Really whines this time, an apology the egg does not accept. The egg did not ask for this. Barely born, and over with, and without and without, a mother.

Proofless of so much as its favorite poem.

Thanks to nature. "Thanks be to God."

"Amen."

The trunk ruptures. It's a mournful, shrill apology. It echoes in homes up and down the street, and even in the cabin on the cruise ship, where the egg's grandparents lie, making love.

(Now that I've written myself out of char-
acters and out of the poem completely, I
think it's time for Mom to come home,
officially.)

(at the house)

(everyone brought vegetarian food)

(even Ditty Boy)

(even Pal's cousin James)

I will never forget when we were kids, and Pal
had that dog with him and how that dog got

us into so much trouble one day. Pal's mama, and it was my aunt, you know, she got after us, man. Because we hadn't been supposed to go down to that creek. Just that creek right back off there, hind Yonah, in those woods.

We hadn't been supposed to go back there, and sure we went, and that dog got all wet and muddy—Nicky was his name. We all got back, and Nicky was dripping mud all over the place, and we got sure enough popping. Well, not the dog.

(eating potato salad with a fork)

(notice how I hold the fork differently, like Mom does)

I had this dream the other night, and, um, you know I got that pump house in the yard. I think you've seen it.

(Ditty Boy points to me)

Well, he was out there. Pal was. In my dream. Believe it or not, he was out there, and it was like he was looking for something. For something to fix something else; and I just said, "What are you doing out here, huh? You big galoot," and he just looked up, and he called me by my real name, which he would sometimes do. He said, "Joe Abel," and then I stepped over, and I . . . I hugged him.

In the kitchen one morning, Pal's silver vat was out. He used it in the shop to melt things, normally. Now he had washed it. He whisked eggs in it. It was a superstition. To eat from it the day of a fishing trip.

"Want to ride out to Ditty Boy's later with me?" he asked as he dunked a piece of white bread.

"Sure," I said. "But what will we be doing there?"

"Catobble-wm-rn," he said. "Catalpa worm run." He turned around. "Oh, you'll see when we get there."

Catobble-wm-rn, or "Catalpa Worm Run": Some dead brush and snapped limbs would

pin upward and scrape the base of the truck as we crunched over them, too

sparse to be woulds [sic], more like a junk-yard of timbs [sic]. Pal would wheez the accelerator, and we'd lurch over one. CRUNCH! He was cackling.

There were chickens in the side yard, all happy and proud. They had a big dead tree trunk to hop onto and off of in the middle of their pen if they wanted. They were eyeing me nd [sic] Pal.

Pal undid the padlock and the chain on the gate [sick]. He draped the chain over his arm as he stomped around to swing it open [sick]. "Punch it," he said, and I punched the accelerator. We were in [sick]. He shut the gate behind us.

[Sick!] [He was sick, Avery!] [Already!] [You could've said something!]

The back field wasn't huge, but there were about a dozen cattle, black-and-white except for one red-colored bull, who Pal said was a new addition. (He said the previous bull had been rotated out, but I didn't want to think about that because I didn't want to think about where the bull had been rotated out to.)

And there were a few calves, one sticking its head between a fence board and a strand of wire to watch us. "Here we go," Pal said, and he marched along the fence to the corner post, where two trees emerged. White grass grew at the roots.

"Catalpa tree," Pal introduced. He bent a limb down. "Take a look."

It was bright-leaved with these toothy-looking seedpods. Pal plucked one.

A catalpa worm is actually a caterpillar that blooms into what's called a hawk moth once it matures.

Pal snatched one up. It would never mature.

He inverted it right before my eyes. I saw the inside of its skin, foam green turned the bright yellow of highlighter liquid.

It stained Pal's hands as he went, setting the worms on a paper towel inside a plastic Tupperware container, side by side.

"It was either me or the birds," Pal said. "Trust me." And when I had a dream, later, about staining a bunch of my sheets bright yellow, I knew what it was about.

I'm sorry it's untitled.

(Luca hands me a mix)

I didn't want to give you something that had a title like "I'm Sorry" or something dumb like that.

It's not all death songs, is it?

(I smile)

(he shakes his head)

No, but it contains my first original. I play guitar on it and everything. A song for you. In the future, though, I might need you to write lyrics because that shit is hard.

TO TUMBLE YOUR WALLS

I remember saying, "Pal! You either got to quit drinking or you got to lose weight!"

(everyone is laughing)

(Mom too)

(I think it's okay)

(we get to know so little about our parents)

(it occurs to me)

(we only get to know them as our parents)

When Mom got home from High Tides, Low Tides, the first thing she planned to do was get groceries. "Okay, so, to buy," Mom dictated, like one of us was writing it down, "uhh . . . bread? Vegetables . . ."

"Do you want to get more specific with the vegetables?" I grabbed a pen and started writing. She was on to things like "batteries."

"Mm, just jot off to the side 'favorite.'" She laughed. She pulled her head back from the pantry. "Honestly, I think the only thing we have left to eat here that isn't expired is the shredded wheat."

"I hate to break it to you. But that shredded wheat is almost definitely expired."

She tossed the box aside. "I don't really want shredded wheat, anyway. Let's have a real breakfast."

We chose a new donut shop that had opened downtown. We shouldn't have. When we got there, they were serving donuts called things like "the cock and balls" in the shape of actual cock and balls.

"Let's get out of here," I said. She said, "Well, hold on a minute." She looked at me like, what is wrong with you? "I want a donut." She was messing with me.

"Mom . . ."

"New restaurant in town, Avery. We gotta support. Yes," she said to the guy at the register, "I think I'll have a voodoo doll, please."

The voodoo doll came jelly-filled, with frosted facial features and a pretzel stick signifying an erect penis.

"My," Mom said. She took out the pretzel and lay it on its side.

"Did you ever want a pet?" (I remember this is one of the early conversations we had after she got back.)

"Yes," I said.

"I would really love a little kitten," she said.

"Would you still love it when it grew into a cat?"

She laughed. "Mm, maybe. Do you remember when that baby bird died out back? Behind the house?"

"I don't think so."

"Remember, we heard something fall, and we went to check. It was that little potted plant we had hanging that Babs gave us and it fell, and there was this little tiny bird inside it, and it was alive."

"I thought you said it died."

"Well, it died later. It couldn't make it on its own, of course. When it did, we buried it."

"Mom, why are you bringing this up?"

"Okay." She stopped. And what was really, really weird, we heard the sound of a potted plant drop, in the distance. We looked at each other. "Time really is a construct," she said. "Everything really is all happening at once."

We forgot about it for a little while, and somewhere in that span of time, a car door closed and an engine cranked. We missed it. Babs was leaving. We finished emptying the fridge. She was gone, she was gone, she was gone.

She had left him—left us.

(when everyone's gone)

Let's get out of here—leave the window up a while. It's hot in here to me. Does it feel hot to you?

(there is still some light left in the evening)

(we walk around)

(I think she wants to talk about Babs)

(maybe I do too)

(but we don't)

Let's do the labyrinth.

At Pal's house: "Dad? Dad, what happened?" Mom called. And I could hear him behind a door, sobbing. "Dad, are you okay?"

"Pal?" I stepped into the hallway. White bread slices scattered along the floor. I walked to the garden room. He was in there. He had the door closed.

"Dad, if you don't open the door, I'm going to break it in just like you did to our back porch that day. Remember?"

It nudged open then. He was posed against the doorframe, looking wobbly, tired, sad, his blue eyes.

Mom and I stepped to either side of him. Vodka smell, like the taste in my mouth the morning after orange drink night. "He's diabetic you know, so." Mom's hands shook as she balanced. "It doesn't take much. I think I, I might be going to be." She looked at me. "Sick, Avery. You might have to—"

I took the full weight of him then. "I was in the kitchen," he started to explain, "making sandwiches. She walked in and just said she was plum leaving me. She didn't say—"

Mom returned. She put a hand up. She stood perfectly still for a few seconds.

"Okay, I think it passed. I think I'm going to make it."

Was it the liquor smell that was getting her? We got Pal over to the couch.

I found towels in the bathroom, brought them out just in case. "You don't have to do this, Ave," Mom said. "Can you bring us some water?" Pal sagged against the armrest. I brought a whole pitcher and cups. We filled a cup for him, and he drank. And Mom drank a cup, and so did I.

It was so dark in the house, so unusual then. "He

needs some good bready food. What would you like to eat, Dad? A turkey sandwich?" He shrugged. His head bobbed. Mom pulled some cash from her pocket.

"Well, what about spaghetti, huh? How does spaghetti sound? Spaghetti sound good? Avery, do we have the stuff for it? Christ, we only need three things." We didn't have three things to make spaghetti. Gia knocked on the door with them later. She stood hugging Mom in the doorway for a while. I cleared the room. They sat down together.

I went into the kitchen to brown the meatless crumbles. Pal was in bed. I wished Luca had come over, and then wondered if all of this was too adult, if Gia had told him not to come. While the meatless crumbles browned, I heard Gia ask Mom if Mom had heard from Babs, and Mom said that no, she hadn't and that she hadn't tried.

Gia left and we woke Pal for dinner. The three of us ate sitting on his bed, watching *A Walk in the Woods*. Pal owned it. He had bought it not too long ago. I think the last movie he bought. He loved Robert Redford, and I liked the movie. I was already seeing the story as some kind of future for Pal once we got through this. A little rougher for the wear, maybe, but still moving.

(there's this place called The Healing Garden)

(in our neighborhood, behind the hospital)

(the labyrinth isn't much)

(takes minutes only)

(little memorials)

(stones)

(angels)

We have to do something like this for him.

We'll talk about it.

I like this one.

(a birdbath with an etching)

(In memory of Billy Stern, please feed the birds)

He'd probably like something more to do
with water.

(Mom laughs)

A buoy on the lake with his name on it.

Exactly. All his fishing buddies will sail by
and be like . . .

They'll say, "There he is."

(we sit a while)

(Mom points)

That one is nice.

(an angel with hands clasped)

(some bird shit on it)

(a placard)

(There are healing angels that walk with us)

It's good to have this place here for people.

"Okay, he drove off!"

"Did you look away?"

"I had to go to the bathroom!"

Mom didn't get angry with me. She just grabbed the keys off the hook. "You coming?" she asked. "He can't be driving if he's drunk."

I didn't know what we'd do if we found him. I

didn't ask. "I'm driving carefully," she told me, "so I need you to keep your eyes peeled. Let me know if you see him."

"Where first?" I asked.

We tried Jay's first, since Jay's was the closest. But he liked that ABC Package Store because of the drive-through.

"Right," I said. I acted like I knew. We turned by the hospital and rolled up toward Jay's. New parking on the side. I could barely see. My hands were shaking. "I don't see him," I said, but knowing it was possible that I'd missed him.

It didn't feel real enough, though. None of it did. We didn't want him to lose control over his own life, so even though we'd gotten rid of all the alcohol in the house, we hadn't asked for his truck keys.

We found him at ABC Package, where there was

a line at the drive-through. We pulled into the gas station across the street and parked up against the edge of the lot. We spied.

"This is what he does," Mom said. "Look." He had done this before; she had witnessed. She had followed him once before, and then followed him right back home. It had made him angry.

He was one car back, and then he was at the window. I made a video in my head. "Vodka," he went, wrongly. The way he spoke. Drawling, tugging on vowels. "Vodka," with its two short syllables and hard consonants, didn't work.

But that's what he ordered. I saw the clear bottle appear in the window, just long enough for me to imagine it dry, and place a ship inside. And then the clear bottle disappeared. Then I saw a bright green bottle appear and then disappear. "What was—"

"Mountain Dew."

The truck went forward a short distance. Pal tipped the Mountain Dew bottle out the driver's-side window. The bright drink fell in a stream, and splashed against the asphalt. "Then he pours the vodka into the bottle," Mom said, when the Mountain Dew retracted, "and mixes it."

There was this woman at High Tides, and she, I'm not supposed to share really, but she was a mom. Is a mom. She had tried to commit suicide, and

I mean, it was so sad, sitting there listening to her. She had bipolar disorder—has bipolar disorder—but she hadn't been diagnosed at that point, and she said that she had the thought:

Okay, so if I just do this, if I just get it over with.

She loved her kids, but she was saying sometimes how like her body couldn't, you know, let her love them.

So it was like if she could just get rid of the body, then all the love she felt would finally be free to just

(Mom waves her hand)

be, you know? Exist in its own right. Free of selfishness and sickness and . . . human stuff.

She was convinced her kids, her babies, would still be able to feel that love without her there, and a better version of it too, that love. And I was just sitting there, listening, thinking about how badly I wanted to come home to you, how I missed you, how I am just so grateful to

be alive, to have you.

There was one night when he called Red Lobster. He placed an order for over $80. He asked Mom to go pick it up.

Mom paid. When we got to the house, I arranged plates on the card table on the porch. We all sat. He'd ordered three lobster dinners, each with a baked potato, side salad, cheddar biscuit, and little plastic cup of melted butter.

"Y'all eat up," he instructed. He forgot we didn't eat lobster. But we ate our baked potatoes and cheddar biscuits and side salads. When she was done, Mom leaned back. The sun seemed to be warming her face through the screen of the porch, and she seemed okay.

Pal ate slowly, wiping his hands with a napkin between each bite. He only spoke once to say, "Good to have a little treat every once in a while, huh?" He never lifted the napkin to his mouth, so some food collected there.

Even though I know I'll like to keep the good days in my memory, I know I'll like to remember him like this too. Having ordered too much from a chain seafood restaurant, with butter on his whiskers, and grunting as he chews. In the grip of his heartbreak, still trying to make us happy.

He wasn't himself after she left. After the Mountain Dew trip, we took his truck keys. He didn't want to come stay with us, and we couldn't stay there. It was almost like a horror movie, walking in. He kept the lights off.

He'd be sitting in his chair. "Partner," he'd go. And I would sit with him, and if he'd made a mess of something, I would clean it up. We brought him each meal and sat at each meal with him. Mom had tried to convince him, but he wouldn't go to therapy. We didn't think he was drinking during this time. We don't think he was.

An old friend would stop in and pay visits sometimes, but really only just one friend. She walked with a cane. Didn't come to the funeral. But she did send a card. It said she was heartbroken. Mom spoke to her a few times. Mostly, she and Pal would just catch up.

She sent a card to us this week too, so it's been a year.

It says she is still heartbroken, that she thinks of him every day. I don't know much about her and Pal's relationship, even now. It got murky for me. The depth of the past, of relationships, of sickness. His days. It did get too adult. I couldn't fathom it. Just the depth of it all.

If I started to try, it started to hurt me. I had to stop. I just worked on what I'd learned. Two feet on the floor. To be present, be. Listen when he was talking to me. To go along with him thinking that I didn't know a thing about what was going on. To let him believe I was still protected from it.

(From what?
How bad life
gets?)

Some advice from Pal:

"Why make a plastic jig silver? Well, I'll tell you. Silver is one of the most successful colors for specifically the bad days, and by bad days, I mean the dreary days. The gray days. Days when the fishing ain't going to be any good, and you're out there trying anyway because that's just how it worked out, you know?

"I realize it might seem contrary to make a gray jig for a gray day. But truth is, the darker the color you use on a gray day, the better."

Luca said one day, "I guess life doesn't level out the way you think it will, ever." Because the thing is, you always have a body. And with it, you have need, you have desire, and you have love, and it all changes.

As we live. Changes.

The matter we're made of, that connects us to stars, in constant motion.

And all of that, even after the body quits, still changing. Disappears here, reappears there. Some nights I can't sit still. He had that too.

He had one really good weekend left. We went fishing. He was lucid.

One night he fell.

THE LONG POEM

"Susannah, if you please,

    What are the messages?"

"The messages are: There

    Are no messages."

    "But the light is blinking. I can see

the light—" "Oh wait, yes. The messages

are,

    Wait here, okay, wait right here, just

while

I'm at the bottom now, please

Hold,

I have to dig for just one minute longer—

Would you like to choose your hold music?"

        "I'd like a Beatles song: specifically
'A Day in the Life,' like when it goes super
Metro—crescendo—and then halt!"
        "We're in it now." "Okay, thanks,
Susannah."

"You are welcome, dear Avery."

"First un-left message

        —"

"Hello, Avery, it's Babs.

I just want to say first, that my note from

you made me cry, and I wanted to say too,

that, even though

I know

You knew,

I mean,

How could you not sense it? Things were

off,

Between Pal and me, and so of

Course you knew, and

shouldn't/couldn't/wouldn't

Ask me rightly to apologize

(Which you didn't, and I appreciate) or cast

blame

(You didn't), but I

Do wish we had more time to talk—

       I'd been preparing some things to say,
and so

Now to just say them to you,

       Just to be happy, and to know that
you're valuable.

I spent so much of my adult life unhappy,
and

       With Pal, it was always hard to get a
word in edgewise.

       Him with that radio going,
'—*always!*' '—*always!*'
       '—*always!*' and always speaking to

Everyone we ran into. Never a

moment's peace,

Oh, and I know those things got to

you too,

Got on your nerves too, but, Avery, oh,

You are younger!

And my life is . . . well, you

Understand. I couldn't spend any more of it

Un—" *(doot)*

"Are you sure you would like to

delete this message?"

"Yes, please. Thanks, Susannah."

"Next un-left message:

—"

"Hi, Avery, it's Mom,

Oh don't mind me, I'm just calling
you from
Ha-wa-ii . . . No, kidding. Well, not really
I'm not 'kidding,' because I am in
Fact, calling you from Hawaii, though it
might as well be

The Arctic here, Avery. I miss you so
badly,
I mean, it might as well be stone-cold
winter—" *(doot)*

"Are you sure you would like to
delete this message?"
"Yes, please.

     Thanks, Susannah."

"No more messages:

     —"

     "Thanks, Susannah." (She's really
not supposed to play me those, so it means a
lot.) "No problem, dear Avery." (It's a risk
she runs because she cares.)

Night is close, but no closer to nothing, so
Are you speaking my language yet?

To go outside: it's funny about the streetlamp
lights,

And the moths, they don't, like, get hot?
        Burn, even? What is worse than
burning,
        can you imagine? Being young is like
being a moth, or alive I
bet—possibly:
        I am burning, if I am learning any-
thing these days, it is that

The flames you keep touching when you're young,
you keep right ahead on touching when you're older

Look at that one, he goes and *tee*—
        Just a slight little tap on the wings on the
warm, off the warm on the wings, and then—

alights suddenly,

Back on again. Everything in
nature
as cyclical as this. Everything in nature

such addiction,

like today, you know how
we sleep with the window
in the bathroom down

& the screen still up;

& you know, sometimes an insect
will get behind the screen & through
somehow:

This morning, a wasp

Yellow striped & brown orange—

& some red—

so much brighter when you really *look*

clawed in

combs antennae behind the mirror

That is prayer:

                              that is mental,

overtaking

the body.

That's distress for you: externa-

mental, at its base

a physical, a coping

mechanism,
an "everything is fine"-

anism.

Animism—

so sad,

makes me sadder than anything.

To think how I left it there
all morning.

I get a drinking glass and an old slip

of paper—

A scrap on which I wrote the make

and model of the toilet seat—

oblong oyster—

when we needed to know.

I slip it beneath the wasp.

I carry it out.

I set it on the grass. It clings to the

inside

of the glass, it encircles

the rim, doesn't go anywhere—

       "a watched pot doesn't boil," I think,

"a cliché"

"is a coping"

"mechanism"

"animism"

"mechanism-animism"

"is belief in the soul of the process"

"mechananimism"

"is belief that a machine"

"has a soul"

—"

When you're old you die, and no other
consolation.

It is true too of the young sometimes—
we die. But I've been watching too many
shows lately where the kids just go out
and party

and listen to how I say "kids" as though I'm
not one
anymore, like this summer totally rent me of
"kids," like I don't want to party:

I'm partying now for crying out loud: this

orange in my cup in my hand, is light orange,

if you

                              catch my drift.

And there are no cars. It is

too late, already, for cars: At 16,

I don't have to think much about family, at

least not

        in terms of starting one;

Though, to be fair, my mom was hardly

        out of high school when she had me

(in her belly, under graduation robes).

        I wonder about how one, say, "gets

there"

"from here"—okay, so, for instance

       this dad along the way down here,
and I see him on his bike sometimes.

He rides up and I don't see a mom or
       another dad ever, and so he does it
His whole life, parenting, et al., alone, but like
how does he get there? To the point where he
can even

Do that? After some kind of shattering?
       What I'm asking is, from where
Do you get the strength?

I walk that way to catch a bit of
       the light the color inside the house
makes.

Lava lamps are making a comeback,

no TV light flickering, so nobody

awake, &

The light is dim enough that it

goes hand in hand with noticing. I

think:

A body needs to sleep.

I am trying to learn.

I do wish my body, like a schedule, a dad

could make.

Sleep at night, work during the day and

make a life that

I am proud of?

Having gone through a shattering, it would

be easy

to do, I imagine. Deserve

A happiness,

       having shattered; it is easy to

Accept.

What I'm saying is that, if I am learning

anything

these days, it is that the buildings in the

craters of

the bodies of adults are there as a conse-

quence of

a shattering. Which they are then forced to

locate,

and then build into, out of, on top of.

And it's how you make a life, accept a

       happiness.

    What I'm

asking is: Am I shattered enough already,
or am I

shattering? (And when do I start to build?)
Maybe

If I keep it at a distance, say,

      as far as my hand is from my mouth,
While I'm holding the orange vodka
drink,

      well, maybe I'll get struck by light-
ning instead. When I stretch out my palm, I
can feel the potential.

      But I contract it again, worried: If
I am learning anything, it is that bitterness,
in younger years, crystalizes and then
sweetens:

forms a rock candy base, which then, when you're older,

rots your teeth. And then they replace your teeth with,

guess what, more rock. More rot. The logic being to replace

rot with rot, to cancel it out. It is the circle of life. To own

the sickness first. Like with bodies. Antibodies. Fight rot with rot.

I.e., beat it to the punch.

"You have rock candy teeth, old man."

I saw the nurses' reactions, pleased, one less thing to clean.

I want pink rock candy for my teeth when I am old,

so everyone will know I'm still queer,
and haven't lost it.

                    "You are really *rough*!"
Remember
When John Wayne said that in *The Searchers*
                    to the young man whose eyes
were so blue:
I was falling in love. I was falling in love, and
                    you were cracking up,
And I was just eyeing the man with his shirt
off.

Replace what rots with rot, and what's rotten is
fixed! It's ingenious, except it keeps perpetuating:
like in family,

Sometimes I do feel like there are two of me in here. I think everyone I know has lost someone, or, at least, like me and Luca, was born missing someone.

Ms. Poss lost both of her parents when she was younger: Can you imagine?

She had no siblings, so it was like she suddenly became the only one to carry all their stories, meaning

The stories they told and the stories they were, but she wouldn't ever tell them, not even to herself, because they made her sad. She said she barely even grieved. And then in college, she went to this art show, a performance, and the artist said, "Under your seats, there is a lighter. Now, hold it up if you've ever lost somebody."

Ms. Poss held up her lighter, and then she wailed. She wasn't the only one wailing. She says

She's convinced that art can heal both the artist and the witness.

She said that my poems might be suffering from over-condensing. I need to let my poems breathe a little.

Well, I have brought this one outside, Ms. Poss. Does that count?

I like a book that makes you do things with your body, like a *Peter Pan*, when you're clapping to keep Tinker Bell alive:
"Dear reader, will you clap your hands with me?"
[Keep my grandpa alive?]

Oh and speaking of old movies, "You're tearing me apart!" That's from *Rebel Without a Cause*, speaking of other old movies with a (then) suggestion of queerness.

"You're tearing me apart!" he roars at his parents. Because they are, but not really. I mean

Jim is a privileged, hot, white teen.

In fact, what tears him apart is the way he sees his dad as castrated by his mom. It's weird, so then tie that in

To evolution, and Jim's dad "should have been gay," as Katy Perry said once about an ex in a song called "Ur So Gay," before she sang a song later about kissing a girl, which was problematic for other reasons.

I mean, imagine being

torn apart by two

People

Parents.

It's funny, *Rebel* starts with Jim at night, in the street. He is wasted and lying on the ground nudging a little toy monkey playing cymbals. And Jim is cool.

People fall in love with Jim.

A queer boy and a straight girl, both.

Before the film ends.

Guess which one dies.

And Jim is in the street at night, drunk, alone, party, like me, when we meet him. I am cool, or at least, I am not doing anything that Jim wouldn't do.

This street is mine. I almost wrote, "it's my street," but that didn't quite do it. That didn't quite convey. The streetlamp lights, except for the bold dark square at the end of the block, where a man in a house once raised hell

about light pollution.

He had left a city once, already, he explained. He didn't want to leave again.

"Out of the frying pan,

                     & into the

           —?"

You know, Luca told me one time that he lucid-dreamed. I do not believe it for a second, because of the way he said the lucid dream went.

He had this realization within the dream that he was dreaming and he started to move stuff with his hands, allegedly, like he was telekinetic.

Now doesn't that seem a little too "on the nose"?

I can't even remember my dreams most of the time, much less control them. I can control a poem, though. Look:

k   !

L

o

o

Have you ever heard the joke, How do
    you make a poem dance?
Well, it's easy but you have to play
    some music, so right now, we'll
Choose "Afterlife" by Arcade Fire, because
    it's about death, and getting through,
But it helps to forget about the lyrics.
    Press play:

I don't know what the instrument is,
    but it sounds like tiny car horns.
I can't teach you and dance to it at the same time,
    so here goes:

                    A aa e

    Ae e

              Ae   a

    Really, it's not even that impressive.

Nothing cummings didn't already do,

    but it's hard for me to fully let go when I'm being

watched.

The chorus:

" Aae

eeaabogado

(abogado, abogado)

  — swim.

 Did you know that there is nothing

  after life? "

Okay, I am really sorry, this is actually a hard song
to do.

 For what it's worth, I am literally dancing
In the street now, like a "kid,"

 I am shattering. I am thinking

We all tote around a rot, a sorrow—

    In our bodies, like a

Puberty.

    When do I get mine, if I haven't—

And I hope (how did you get yours?)

    That I have? What I am saying is—

like in *Peter Pan*—

The issue is not (really) growing up too soon.

You know what the best use of the word "kids" I

can think of is? That MGMT song, "Kids," and they

don't even say it in the song, it's just the song's name:

    and the song is more about nature like all the best

art is: I want to believe in something bigger

    Maybe that is what happens when you shatter: a

belief in something bigger. You let a light in; you can't help it. You emerge a sudden believer, and a-sudden, you have the strength that it takes to build.

> Hey, look at nature.
> No, look at it.
> Every time I start to, I get self-conscious: But
> there are so many *things* in nature to see,
> and I've not seen a-one, and now
> It is dark out,
> And everywhere

Are wasps,

> and I am living hand to mouth in
> the mouth of the dull orange drink.

> But if I finish I can set it down.

What I am asking is: Did I shatter my mom?

A cat!

A black cat.

Hey, you're a black cat, not meant to be a bad omen, I hope—nah, I don't believe in that.

Though you are the crow of the land.

But, now you're gone!

Well, that's why I like cats I guess. They play you.

"You are really *rough*!" I call after it. Like life,

I don't mean

To laugh,

Or death.

I mean,

I like a text that makes you do things,
physically.

Lets you know that you're alive.

Like, remember in *Peter Pan*, that scene
when the narrator asks you

To clap if you believe in fairies—

To save Tinker Bell from dying?

[Did I ask you this already?]

And you do?

You clap.

I mean, [I clapped].

What I'm asking is:

[Could you clap to save my grandpa from
dying?]

But no—I didn't.

No, I won't ask.

Because what if you didn't, or don't.

And what if you felt, or feel, bad for not doing so?
Or it doesn't work, and so you question your beliefs.

No, it is too much to ask,

But I didn't ask it

[clap, clap, clap away]

anyway.

In high school sometimes,
A boy walks down the hallway

And other boys start clapping.

"Clap if you believe in fairies!"

It's oft-quoted. "Clap if you believe!"

But I'll be a fairy,
any day. So long as I never have to grow old
and get rock candy teeth.

"You're tearing me apart!"

That's just the way of it.

1. Oh another thing I think about, periodically

2. About *Peter Pan*, is how

3. The mom learns about Peter when she's arranging her kids' heads at night

4. while they sleep.

5. But she doesn't bring it up with them later: It's

6. Against the code of moms.

7. But it's necessary because how else is

8. A mom supposed to know what's troubling her love?

9. Words like "F—"—and "DAD"—and "PETER" appear.

10. I'm awake now,

11. And I'm sensing she has rummaged.

12. Because she's calling me.

13. Susannah rings.

14. I answer,

15. "Hello?"

16. "Hello, Ave?"—and by the way she says it

17. I can tell it's wrong,

something worse than we

18. "They're telling me it's, uh"

19. "he has zero brain, uh, activity"

20. "he is only living"

21. "by machine."

What happened is he fell, my Pal, and then he stopped being able to speak:

First, confusion of words: his first wife's name for his girlfriend's. Then girlfriend's name for his mom's. Then "sky" for "water," "bait" for "breath."

Then the invention of words: "feefer" for remote control, "REFAMA LAG TAN ME!"—that kind of thing.

"And I, I just wanted to ask you"—she clears

her throat—"do you want to come say goodbye? You don't have to, and I'm scared to leave. But maybe Gia can drive you, or Luca? If

"you don't want to involve them, I understand. If you don't want to say goodbye

"I understand. You were with him in his last good days. You may not even feel like you need to. You were

"with him already." But I want to, I do, to say goodbye. "I want to," say.

"So I will call Gia, to come give you a ride." "Mom, no, don't worry about calling her. I can call her. I will get there, don't worry."

"They said they'll take him off support around three, and when they do that, he could

he could go instantly, or he could," she hangs on, "it could even be, it's "sometimes"

"days."

"I'll be there."

"And if you could look in his shop for some things, if

you, if you have time, maybe his favorite book." He has

two, though. Which one? He has

22. *The Compleat Angler* by Izaak Walton and

23. *A River Runs Through It* by Norman Maclean

24. And I will bring along "The Fish" by Bishop too.

". . . we're just sitting here," she explains, "in the quiet, and the sound of the respirator is"

—"

I tell her I will grab the book and be there as soon as I can be.

"It was because of the

medication he was taking."

She keeps explaining. Like doctors are explaining it

all to her right now, as she relays it to me

on the phone, in real time: before it's processed (a shattering):

"It thinned out his blood. It was that
mixed with the alcohol that caused the

bleeding." It
thinned out his blood.

That, mixed with the alcohol, caused the bleeding, the
medication, for

diabetes, McFlurries hidden
in the shop freezer, the secrets, the fact of

(". . . not just the drinking . . . the lying, the
deceit . . . inherited . . . !")

as though to say,

    whose fault? that led to

    —"

25. Be honest about how you feel

26. With the people you love

27. Who love you

28. Who are worth it.

29. I am feeling love for Mom right now, and so much sadness.

30. I tell her so, her only father.

31. "I'm so sorry."

32. She is feeling love for me too, and sadness

33. And helplessness and uncertainty and fear.

34. She tells me so.

35. Even the hard stuff.

36. That's how it goes, my best friend.

—"

I go to the window—Pal's house sits empty and dark—His garage door is up—

I spot a mirror-me in there—Faceup on the floor, and what aches in my right knee aches in his left— What's in the front of my brain is in the back of his—He thinks less about Pal dying—But if I add some weight and age—60 years—I see, it's Pal there—lying.

How's my meter? How's my—

rhymin'?—God, nauseated—from the dull orange—I stagger over—

to the sink—catch water in my hands—swivel it around—Keurig shoots black coffee straight onto the countertop—forgot to put the mug down—I crutch in—

to the bathroom—slide into the tub—burn my

eyes with Mom's face wash—decide I can stand without crutch, so then slide up, out the tub—along, to the gaping rim—

—oblong, oyster—

and fall in—

to the bowl—I forgot to put the seat down.

I'm losing it again.

The phone rings.

Susannah gets it.

37. "Hey, Ave, it's Luca. I know you're probably getting ready now"

38. "I'm so sorry about this. I—"

39. "If you want to call me or just come on over when you get this"

40. "I've got the car. I'm good to drive you."

—"

Pal's neighbor Mrs. Shivens stands by the gutter—with her dog, Banjo—Banjo wears a black bandana—Mrs. Shivens's husband passed away this March—story goes, Banjo barked as they interred the body—I wave at them and smile—

I'm a little paranoid I still seem drunk—"Going

to be a hot one!" she calls over—I pretend I don't hear—Hard to do passing conversation with a party on crutches—Takes too long to pass—so I stall.

"Going to be a hot one"—Two beats—"Pardon?"—again. "Oh, yes!" I agree finally—close enough.

      When I crutch with long strides—I do it to the chorus of

      "Chandelier"—hold it in my head while—

      "iiiiiiiiii" marks one stretch—"want to swiiiiiiiiing" marks two—
      "from the chandliiiiiiiier" marks three—"from the chandeliiiiiiiiier," four—

      —"

41. A spare key is in the clay pot

42. On the front porch

43. Beneath a bed of soil with a leafless wooden stem.

44. You have to grab the stem to release the soil,

45. All compacted in a grainy, soggy block.

46. Then there's the trick of the lock. Since the dead bolt jams.

47. Harder to do when it's muggier out, when the wood frame expands.

48. In the foyer now

49. Where he fell.

50. To my left hanging from a metal wire hook is

51. The one hanging planter she left behind.

(what happened is

she left, and

he fell, and

  what happened is,

against the corner of the coatrack

my Pal

—"

fell)

"Be present. You have to hurry."

52. Pal's shop key hangs from a peg on the wall
near the hanging dead fern—

53. I grab it.

73. He is on the respirator

74. But soon he'll be off it.

75. —," is precisely the sound it makes.

76. —," —," —," —," —," —"; it's constant.

77. When they turn it off, will it go silent?

78. The staff is kind. Two nurses do the work.

79. Mom stacks the books in her lap, in order of importance.

80. "This is the one," she says, setting it on top.

81. And then removing it.

82. And then setting it on the bedside table.

54. The blueberry bush out back has a spanworm

55. Infestation, so no blueberries will grow this
July.

56. Paint chipped above the doorknob

57. And the floodlights to his little shop on, like

58. I left them; too sad to leave dark.

59. I unlock and stumble, send the green
ottoman

60. On wheels, sailing. Catch myself

61. Against his workbench, the jig molds

62. The shape of little bugs, bodies
curved in-

63. To a point, but no sting.

83. Now is the time.

84. The sound of the respirator,

85. When they turn it off,

86. Does quit.

87. He sits up.

88. His eyes open

89. And mouth.

90. "Oh my—" Mom says.

91. Hands go to her face.

92. A nurse holds her shoulders.

93. "A reflex, a reflex," she says. She is nodding, "That's"

94. "all it is."

95. Mom keeps her head turned.

96. His eyes close again.

97. He settles back down now.

98. "Oh my—" Mom repeats.

64. Pinned to the corkboard, a paper sign I made:

65. *Pal-Made Lures! They're one of a kind!*

66. Nearby, an article, "Local Organization Protests 'Blind Eye' to Global Warming."

67. The sun is warming the water everywhere. It's a problem.

68. There are warmwater fish and coolwater fish, and

69. The coolwater fish are getting confused, their water

70. No longer cool enough, and so they keep moving upward

71. Into the thermocline

72. And dying.

99. There are tubes and things

100. and one of those plastic bags that collects pee hanging off the side.

101. Alibaba brand, of course.

102. Mom slides a chair up next to it.

103. "Okay," she says. She takes a deep breath.

104. Opens to page one.

105. *"In our family, there was no clear line between religion and fly fishing."*

106. Mom closes the book.

107. She turns to me, red-eyed, and shakes her head.

108. "I'm going to need to take a minute, Avery. I have to—"

109. She gets up and crosses the room.

110. I don't know if I should go after her.

111. I don't want to leave him alone.

73. On the floor is an ashtray

74. Filled with plastic jigs he tossed, something wrong with them.

75. This batch brighter colored, for coolwater fish.

76. I stoop to pick it up and drop my crutch.

77. Nudge the cabinet door

78. Open, inside it,

79. A slender blue-neck bottle

80. He squirreled. He drank it.

81. Empty now.

82. Did he simply not want to beat it?

83. I'm oversimplifying, I know.

112. The bathroom door swings shut, down the hall.

113. I pick up the book.

114. *"In our family, there was no clear line . . ."*

115. I interrupt myself to swallow.

116. *"In our family, there was no clear line . . ."*

117. Pal's ragged breath interrupts.

118. *"In our family, there was no clear line . . ."*

119. I pause again.

120. The breathing is really like his snoring, but

121. Strained, rubbed raw-sounding.

122. It sounds like it hurts.

123. Occasionally, speeds up,

124. Gets louder,

125. So loud it's difficult to believe

126. He can hear me.

127. I can look at him.

128. He once said, "Sometimes it feels
like you been around my whole life,
partner,"

129. "and sometimes it feels like you was just
born yesterday."

84. I take the books from the bookshelf.

85. I un-pin a copy of the poem.

86. It is stuck to a paper fishing guide

87. Pal wrote, actually. A little manual with a
stapled spine.

88. It slides to the floor.

89. I scoop it up.

130. I can tell by the sounds of his breathing,
though he is off the respirator,

131. Though his brain activity is zero, that he is
my Pal.

132. There are still the things you don't normally see in other people, unless

133. You're like me right now,

134. Sitting across a gray room from them

135. While they're dying,

136. Such as

137. The way the skin looks smoother, more aired out, against the face,

138. The way the hand sometimes flutters, as though discarding pocket lint,

139. The way the chest and throat and mouth

140. Work to give and give, everything

141. Saying, "I am giving up." It doesn't

142. Look effortless, by a stretch.

143. It looks brave.

144. Which I can qualify,

145. Saying he is brave.

146. Someone who raised me,

147. Who loved me.

from "The Angler's Guide to Fishing with Heart" by Paul Avery "Pal" Fowell

THE BASICS:

CASTING

1. Hold → hold the line with index finger to prevent line from flowing off the spool, with the bail open

2. Bring → the rod will "load"

3. Stroke → release the line midway through toss

4. Feather → stop the line with index finger
when it hits target,

> then flip the bail over the spool

148. Two feet on the floor

149. Board.

150. Pal flicks the blinker up.

151. Old wooden fence posts

152. Turned gray.

153. We ride by.

154. I choose the pop song every time.

from "The Angler's Guide to Fishing with Heart"
by Paul Avery "Pal" Fowell

<u>THE BASICS</u>:

LANDING

1. Land the fish quickly, and keep the handling of the fish to a minimum.

2. Remove the hook from its mouth before taking it from the water, or use wet hands.

3. To remove the hook, use pliers or another hook with the barb pinched down.

4. If the fish swallows the hook, just cut the line. Fish possess strong digestive enzymes, which will dissolve the hook in time.

5. If you need to revive a fish, rock it gently back and forth in the water. It will swim away when ready.

6. When its gills begin to move again, you may then release it.

155. "When you were born, and I went

down the hallway, to the room where you were,"

156. "with that big glass window, and all those babies are crying,"

157. "and there you were, and you were perfect."

158. "And I just cried and cried, because from that point on"

159. "I had a new friend"

160. "only just been born. And he'd hung the moon already."

***

SURVIVED BY

Back home from the hospital, Mom goes straight to bed. I think about how this bodes.

          Straight to bed—is that how it goes? Mom would know, I reckon, having already lost one parent.

      Get home and it's straight to bed, or it's straight to booze, straight to church, whatever—and since the seal got broken, and someone has slipped out—all things go whirring by. (Yet you remain—and I.)

I knock on your door. I say, "I love you, Mom, I'll see you in the morning"—and we'll begin to wait it out, you—and I, we'll wait it out.

THE BLUE HOUR

Luca and I go on walks and chart the rotting of the station wagon in the lot by the corner of the block. Blue grass knotting in its tires, hubcaps vamoose.

It's been a good walking summer. This summer. I've been carrying a camera—that's what Ginsberg did. The station wagon is Luca's favorite thing, and we chart the degradation of it; at the same time, his growth. He always poses beside it. He promises not to cut his hair, the whole summer. So we'll document the progress: the process.

It's been a good cat summer too. We counted eleven cats one evening, while walking. Today so far, four.

Right behind the station wagon, a modern home is getting built. A tall cuboid with long windows and wood-paneled walls. "I want to go inside there," Luca says. "Do you?"

I do. It's so at odds with everything on our street. "I don't know why we haven't done this before. The door isn't locked." He turns the knob. "And there's nothing in here yet, so we're obviously not trying to steal."

I agree with Luca. If they were worried about trespassers, they would keep the door locked.

It's three floors, including a basement. We stare out the windows of the main floor, the middle. It's dusk, so the sky is pink. Luca says, "Hey, let me get a picture of you." I stand at the window, and he takes one. I look at it. I'm a ghost backed by purple light in it

dead, true. But it's been a good cat summer.

"I like it," I say. I was a ghost backed by purple light. "It's weird," I say, "you know, like there's no soul here yet."

"Exactly."

"People have to live in it first."

"We could do them a favor."

"What are you thinking?" I ask.

"Add some soul."

He smiles.

The basement. Loose tiles on the floor, and so

much white dust. It looks like where chalk dust goes to die, along with wood shavings. We're stripped so our moms won't know. The clothes on the stairs leading down.

There's a bizarro Krystal to-go coffee cup buried in dust. Unidentifiable foam chops, of insulation, white & pink fluff. The dust is really something severe. Mounds against wood frame like leaves to dive in.

We won't. But maybe. His ass is what you call "bubble." Everything else is even better than what you call that.

He kisses me. "It's unlocked," I say.

"Not," he says, bounding up the stairs, "—for long!" I keep my underwear on. I snap a picture of him when he gets back.

"Confidential!" he demands. And we kiss. And where do we lie? Right on the floor. We push ourselves through dust. Ass scratches. Knees, scratches. My teeth graze the bone of his hip. We deem it

worthy. Took the year to get here. I'll kiss you. I'll kiss your neck, kiss your thigh. Get the camera out: of here:

it's been a good cat summer: cats on car roofs, in windows, in beds of straw: and in fact, in this last year, something miraculous happened.

Luca happened upon a small cat, barely a kitten but still, like the last to leave the nest, whose mother had died. Luca knew because the kitten was at the mother's side. I wrote a "threnody" in honor of her. I dedicated it to Luca. A "threnody" is a song or a poem for someone who has died. And I like the word, how it looks like "nobody."

I haven't shown it to him yet, still need to revise:

"Threnody to a Mother Cat"

for Luca

When I asked Mother was she afraid,
she said she was not. "My only fear is
that it will be a *vegetarian* feast," she
said. She laughed and licked the sore
spot where it had grown.

Some nights ago I'd asked her if she
believed in the man who kept coming

around. He would always be stirring my tail, and I would wake up and hiss, and then he would stop and beam; he was smug and an annoyance, and by the light of his head, I never got to sleep.

"My dear, hrrrr," Mother said, "of course I do. That is Saint Francis, my sweet. He has to come around."

"Why does he have to come around?"

"Because one of us," she said, "is getting very old."

I am, I thought. *Getting very old. I will be seven months soon.*

Saint Francis came the next night. He stirred his finger next to my tail. I decided every time the tail flicks and it is not my intent, then it is him. Mother said he *could* go invisible if he wanted.

"Like we might do hunting or do climbing or do knowing, Saint Francis might go invisible."

She yawned.

"He might also be a good hunter, if he chose to be," she added, "but he chooses not."

"Why does he choose not?"

"Because, hrrr," Mother said, "Saint Francis loves all the animals."

I woke Mother when I woke one night fidgeting, and felt bad.

Saint Francis was there. "Only in dreams," he said knowingly, "from now on."

Mother gave two hurt, quiet hiccups. "Hrrrr," she said.

I lay my head high near her shoulders. There were divots on her body, into which pain pooled.

She tried more to sleep. "You tell me, sweetheart."

"Tell you what?"

"I can, I can," she said.

"She doesn't want to do it now," I said to Saint Francis. "She can't."

"Not since I gave birth," Mother said.

"And how long ago," I asked, to prove that Mother and I were neither that old, "was that?"

"Years," Mother answered, tiredly. "How many years, Saint Francis? I can't . . ." But Mother never forgot before.

"Six months," Saint Francis answered. "She is only six months old. A whole life ahead of her. Just tell me when, sweetheart . . . You've done only good here, brought nothing but goodness and light and love into this world."

"And when I go, it doesn't go?" she asked.

"Oh, heavens no," Saint Francis said.

(I hissed at him. He was making it happen.)

"And it is true about the feast?" Mother asked. "And I can eat meat?"

"Yes, it is true."

"And true about my loved ones holding me? Holding more than just the memory of me?"

"Yes . . ."

"Because you know, just like I know, that memory is fallible. And there is something else, something after?"

"Well, obviously," Saint Francis said.

"And it is true we reconnect in time?"

"You cannot reconnect when you have never been apart."

"I can, I can," Mother said.

And I said, "Mother, you can," and it was horrible, and it was hard, and I wept—I am still weeping.

I am still weeping, even as the boy comes up and crouches down next to Mother.

Saint Francis is holding me, keeping me still. I am invisible in St. Francis's arms. "Ready now?" Saint Francis asks me. "I can let you go."

"I can, I can," I weep, and am let go, and am crying as I circle the body of my mother and investigate—*Can you hear me?*

"It is more than hearing," Saint Francis says.

But I am not ears right now, not hearing. I need to be left alone. And he obliges me—he's gone.

The boy waits until I am done checking on Mother. Then he scoops me up.

Months passed before I could run. When the summer hit, I was running every day.

I put on gym shorts and sometimes no shirt and hit the road. One morning Mom woke up and said, "I feel like singing." And so she went to church. She went with Gia. I didn't go, and Luca stayed with me, thinking we'd give them both some time.

Gia called after church and said they were staying for Sunday school, but could Luca pick up something for lunch. He left to go grab us all something and I stayed home:

It comes out of nowhere, except that I am reading beside the window. I put the book down. It hits me.

I miss you. I wish you were here.

I let it hit me, and it hits me hard.

I'm not scared of the feeling. It has shown up, and I am facing it. I let everything happen, and I am facing it.

I let everything happen as it's supposed to.

I lean forward and brace my head against the windowsill. It is cool against my brow line.

Like a hand testing for fever.

A thing a parent does.

A reminder: I'm here, I'm here.

At the corner of the sill, the thin fold where shadow meets wall

I whisper—

I know you are. I can feel you. I put on gym shorts.

I put on "Afterlife." I go running to it, nonstop. For a long time, I go—

I think, a high (a runner's).

I think, *Hi!*

I think, *Heaven.*

I don't turn around. If I don't turn around, if I don't see them (if I don't not see them), then how will I know they're not (and even if I did, and didn't see them) there.

Pal, Mom, Luca, Gia, Ms. Poss.

Even Sia, the singer, because why not? Even Sia, the cat. Even her mother cat. Even Anne, Sylvia, John Berryman,

Allen G., and the others.

Even if they all file in toward the back

of the "pack,"
of the "heap,"
of the "family,"
my family

ongoing,

they're

there,

there,

there.

Acknowledgments

This book was written in memory of three people: my Nana (*1944–2015*), my Pop (*1942–2013*), and my Granddad (*1932–2015*).

To my aunts and uncles and cousins, to my brother and sister, to my Mom and Dad—I love y'all so much. I think that's what drives me to write at all.

To David Levithan for your eyes, ears, heart— and for your fearless devotion to this book.

To Sabrina Orah Mark for shining a light in a dark tunnel.

To Peter Knapp for your patience, counsel, and good faith.

To Baily Crawford for your vision.

To Rachel Watkins and Sarah Baline and Caitlin Baker and Johanna Albrecht and Caleb Zane Huett and everyone at the *Commonplace: Conversations with Poets and Other People* podcast.

To Erin Lovett, of Four Eyes, for writing the song "St. Francis Loves All the Animals."

To Sarah Cossart for seeing me—no, finding me—when I was 17.

To my cat Olive, who runs into the bedroom every morning and jumps onto my lap to wake me up.

To Tyler Goodson for every day.

To my Grandma, who gave me an important book of poetry when I graduated from high school. She left a note on the inside: "Don't ever forget those who love you."

I won't forget, Grandma—I love you.

Thank you.

About the Author

Will Walton is a bookselling, pop music fanatic who grew up on a farm. He's a graduate of the University of Georgia, and currently lives in Athens, Georgia. His first novel, *Anything Could Happen*, was a Lambda Literary Award finalist.